LAURIE FARIA STOLARZ

RETURN TO THE DARK HOUSE

HYPERION

LOS ANGELES · NEW YORK

Printed in the United States of America
First Hardcover Edition, July 2015
First Paperback Edition, July 2016

10 9 8 7 6 5 4 3 2 1
FAC-025438-16155
Library of Congress Control Number for Hardcover Edition: 2015006630
ISBN 978-1-4231-9473-6

Visit www.hyperionteens.com

Just when I thought my nightmares couldn't get any worse, I woke up to face the reality of my life.
—Ivy Jensen

RETURN TO THE DARK HOUSE

Dear Parker,

Years ago, after my parents were killed, my therapist thought it would be a good idea to write them letters—as many as I felt I needed to, for all of the things I wanted to share.

She told me that I should write the letters on special paper, seal them up in envelopes, and then mail them to myself, so that one day, years later, I could open the letters and see how much I'd grown.

The idea seemed stupid to me at the time. I was angry, confused, incapable of perspective, never mind growth. But I really don't know what else to do here, Parker. And so I'm going to write you letters, starting with this one, but not as a way to track my growth, and not because I think you're dead.

I'm just hoping to feel connected to you.

It's been almost two months since the Dark House, and in that time, the FBI has come up with only a few basic theories—or at least only a few they're willing to share with me. First, that aside from you and Taylor, all of the other contest winners were killed at the amusement park.

I don't think that's true. They have yet to uncover a single body. That theory is based solely on my testimony about the movie clips we saw just before my escape. Well, that and the amount of blood discovered at a few of the nightmare rides.

The second theory is that the person in charge has an unlimited supply of money.

I know, not exactly rocket science, right?

Everybody keeps telling me to move on. But how can I move anywhere when you and the others are still missing? I know it may sound dumb, but after my parents' death, I never really allowed anyone to get too close—not my foster family, not one single friend—for fear that person might get taken from me too. But then I met you, and I broke all my own rules by allowing myself to be vulnerable and letting you in.

The time we spent together was the closest I'd felt to anyone in years. And, just as I'd always feared, you were taken from me too. But I'm going to get you back. And years from now when I open this letter, hopefully you'll be sitting right beside me, and I can share it with you for real.

Love always,

Ivy

LATE SUMMER

IVY JENSEN

MY BEDROOM DOOR CREAKS OPEN, AND THE LIGHT
from the hallway penetrates my room. I see his boot first: black
wrinkled leather, soiled at the toe.

My gaze travels up his leg. He's wearing a bright-red suit, as
part of his elf costume, along with a floppy hat and green gloves.

He stares at me in the doorway with his tiny, dark-gray eyes:
they're rimmed with amber-brown; I'd recognize them anywhere.
His silver hair is just as I remember it too—thick, shoulder-length,
and wavy, tied back in a low ponytail, and with thin strands of
black coursing through it.

"Good evening, Princess," he says. His tongue inches out of his mouth, between his crooked yellow teeth, in the creepiest of grins. He looks around the room—at my soccer banners, my music posters, and all of my touches of pink—before meeting my eyes again. "It's *very* nice to see you."

There's a cut on his face, just below his eye, extending four inches down his cheek. A trickle of blood runs from it, dripping onto my paisley bedcovers. Did my mom scratch him with her fingernails? Did Dad cut him with something sharp?

"Have you enjoyed the gifts I've sent you?" he asks. "The star pendant? The makeup kit?"

My fingers trembling, I reach inside my bag, searching for Taylor's cell phone. I go to click it on, only to discover that it's a calculator, not the phone.

The Nightmare Elf pulls a knife from the pocket of his suit and holds it out for show—a six-inch spring spike with a double-action blade. He brings it up to my neck, points the tip into my throat.

"Please," I whisper, pressing the back of my head against the wall, fighting the urge to swallow.

"Ivy!" Parker shouts. His voice is followed by the sound of glass breaking.

The noise startles me awake. I sit up in bed, out of breath, before realizing where I am.

In my room.

At the hospital.

A clock on the wall ticks. It's only four in the morning.

I touch my neck and try to swallow. It feels like sharp blades inside my throat. I must be getting sick.

Someone else must be up too. I can hear the sound of glass being swept, can picture the broken pieces entering someone's skin.

And that's when I remember.

I push the call button. "I need somebody to come in here!" I shout, despite the fact that my roommate is sleeping only a few feet away. I grab my notebook from beneath my pillow and write down the new clue, hoping I'm not too late.

Ivy

THE TICKTOCK OF THE WALL CLOCK ECHOES THE TICKING deep inside me. My very own personal time bomb, just a sneeze away from going off.

I pinch the skin on my knee, and feel the familiar cramp—a stabbing sensation at the base of my thumb that radiates up my arm, into my elbow, setting my nerves aflame. The cramping is what eventually gets me to stop pinching.

Not the bloodred nail marks in my skin.

Not the black-and-blue blotches over both kneecaps.

Not the shamrock-shaped patch of yellow (a bruise in healing) swimming in a sea of purple skin.

I think I might spontaneously combust if someone doesn't come in here within the next sixty seconds.

Ticktock, ticktock.

The medication isn't working. It's supposed to lighten and dull, but instead it seems to magnify. Everything feels brighter, louder, harsher, sharper.

I'm in one of the private meeting rooms. Sitting among white walls and metal folding chairs, at a laminate table with boogers and gum wads stuck underneath.

Because I started sleeping with knives.

Because Apple and Core, my foster parents, don't think I'm the safest person to be around.

Not safe for myself.

Not safe for any of my foster siblings.

I can't say I blame them. I honestly don't know what *safe* is anymore. I doubt that it even exists.

I drum my fingers against the table to drown out the ticking. My palm aches. The nubs of my fingers feel tingly.

Finally, there's a knock on the door. It creaks open. An officer walks in. Detective Thomas, local P.D. A major letdown. "I'd asked to speak with the FBI," I tell him.

"Nice to see you too." He nods a hello and takes a seat across from me. There are pouches beneath his eyes from lack of sleep. At least we have one thing in common.

I take my notebook from my lap and open it up to the first page. "There are some things we need to go over."

After only a couple of seconds of reading, he lets out a heavy sigh. His breath smells like Cheetos. "We've been through these details before, Ivy. I thought you had something new."

"I do, but first we need to review."

"We've already reviewed." He's looking at me rather than my notes. "We've also explored, dissected, examined, and revisited. Trust me when I say that we're doing all we can."

"Well, it isn't good enough."

"Ivy." His voice softens. "Leave the manhunt to us, okay? That's *our* job. Your job is to get better and then get out of here."

"Have you had a psychologist examine the winning contest essays?" I ask him. "Or analyze our personality profiles to determine how the killer chose us?"

"What do you think?"

"That's why I'm asking." I start flipping forward and backward through the pages of my notebook, pointing out charts and parallels I've drawn.

Detective Thomas indulges me by reading over a chronology

I wrote—my summation of what happened on the Dark House amusement park night.

The second worst day of my life.

But then he closes the cover and slides the notebook across the table at me. "Take care of yourself, Ivy. Get some rest and get yourself better. If we find out anything, we'll let you know." He gets up to leave.

"No!" I shout, getting up too. I flip the notebook back open and scramble to the page marked Unanswered Questions. "Did you find any of the people who helped set up the amusement park? Or how about the drivers who picked us up from the airport... or Midge?"

"The amusement park had been there for years." He sighs again. "It was abandoned and then revived for the Dark House weekend. The same goes for the cabin; someone made it look like the real Dark House. The FBI was able to find one of the drivers and he was brought in for questioning, but it seems he never met the suspect in person, only corresponded with him via text messages and e-mail. Those accounts have since been deleted."

"Okay, so what about all of the creepy voice-overs that were used at the park?" I point to item number seven on the list of unanswered questions. "Do we know the identity of those people?"

"Ivy..."

"It's a valid question."

"It's hard to find someone based solely on a voice—particularly a voice that none of the authorities heard. Need I remind you that all of the audio and visual equipment was gone by the time the officials got to the park? The people who were hired to do those voice-overs probably didn't even know what they were participating in—what the suspect's project was, that is."

"In other words, no one's contacted those people."

Detective Thomas holds up his hands, as if he wants to talk me down off an imaginary ledge. If only I could jump.

"Parker is alive," I snap. "He's going to star in the sequel. The killer is making another movie. What are you doing to stop him?"

"Get better," he says again, stepping back from the table.

"Doesn't anything I say mean anything to you at all?"

"Of course it does. I'm here, aren't I? You asked to speak to the authorities about a new lead in the case. I come all the way down here, and all you have are recycled clues, not to mention well-covered territory."

"The killer has a scar."

The detective's eyes widen as he studies my face, perhaps waiting for me to take the words back. When I don't, he grabs a notebook and pen from inside his jacket and sits back down. "How do you know?"

I draw an invisible line down my face with my finger. "I only remembered the scar recently. It's a diagonal mark that extends from just below his right eye to just above his jawbone."

"Hold on," he says, jotting the information down, "I thought you said before that he was wearing a mask during your nightmare ride. Did he take it off?"

I open my mouth to answer, feeling my face flash hot. A sickly sensation churns in my stomach. Acid burns a hole in my throat. I look back up at the clock—*ticktock, ticktock*—realizing what I've done.

"*Ivy?* Did he take the mask off?"

I shake my head, suddenly feeling like I've morphed into a little girl, caught for stealing from her mother's purse.

"Then how do you know about a scar?"

I bring a strand of hair across my eyes, as if it could possibly hide me. I take a deep breath and travel back in my mind to the instant that I remembered the scar—around four this morning, after having just woken up from a nightmare about my parents, about their killer, only he'd been dressed like the Nightmare Elf from the Dark House case. Parker's voice had called out to me (another Dark House detail). Plus, also in the dream, I'd been searching for Taylor's cell phone (a third Dark House detail).

"Ivy?"

"I'm sorry," I say, shaking my head. "I'd been so swept up in the detail of the scar that I hadn't stopped to question it."

Thomas's furry blond eyebrows knit together in confusion; they look like caterpillars mating.

"I did remember a scar," I tell him. "But it was on the face of my parents' killer from seven years ago. You're right. The Nightmare Elf *was* wearing a mask at the amusement park. He never took it off." I breathe in and breathe out; there's tightness in my chest. "All of the nightmares I've been having . . . they've been colliding inside my head, bleeding into one other. Sometimes it's hard to decipher which details go with which case."

"Don't worry about it." He closes up his notebook. "Stress like this can wreak havoc on the brain . . . distort your sense of reality."

"But it *is* real," I insist. "The scar, I mean. I remember it distinctly. Isn't there a name for instances like this? Repressed memories or something?"

He gets up once again, not dignifying the question with an answer.

"Not yet," I bark, grabbing at the ache in my head. "There's so much more to talk about. Did anyone check out the hardware stores within a twenty-mile radius of the Dark House? Here, I've located three of them." I pull a map from the back pocket of my notebook and open it up; it covers half of the table. "The red X is for the Dark House," I tell him. "The purple one is for the amusement park. The hardware stores are marked with blue X's. The green X is for the Horror House, a tiny one-room theater

16

that's only open at night and only plays scary films. I was thinking that maybe the killer liked to go there."

"I wasn't aware that Internet access was allowed at this place."

"It's not. I've been working on this map since before I got here."

"What are the orange *X*'s for?"

"Electronics stores where he might've purchased video equipment. Maybe one of the shop owners remembers him. Or maybe the shops use surveillance video. Or what about the real estate agent who sold him the Dark House?"

Detective Thomas stares at me with an amused expression, the corner of his mouth turned upward. "I'm impressed. But, as I've said before, you can rest assured that we've got all of these angles covered."

"What about Taylor then?" I persist. "What made her leave the Dark House early?"

"That's of no concern to you right now."

"*Tell me*," I insist.

"All you need to know where Taylor's concerned is that she saw something at the Dark House that alarmed her enough to leave. By the time investigators got to the house, they were unable to find that something."

"What was it? What did she see?"

"Ivy," he says yet again.

I hate my name. I hate my life. I stand in front of the door so he has no choice but to hear me out. "Why won't you help me?" A sob gets caught in my throat. "I mean, there has to be some reason."

"Some reason for what?"

"For why Taylor left. For why you're keeping key pieces from me. For why the two worst experiences of my life are melting together inside my brain, haunting me while I sleep."

Ticktock, ticktock. My whole body's sweating and yet I feel chilled to the bone.

"Step out of the way." There's tension on Detective Thomas's face, scrunched up on his brow.

I secure the knob in both of my hands, behind my back.

"I'm not asking you," he insists.

"Wait," I blurt, the answer finally clicking.

Thomas reaches behind me to grab the knob, but I widen my stance so he can't. "You know you're only going to buy yourself more time in here, don't you?" he asks, lowering his voice. "What good will that do you or any of the missing victims?"

"Like you give a shit about any of us!" I shout. "You've already written them off as dead."

"You leave me no other choice." He goes to knock on the door, but I block his fist with my hand. "The killer knows where I live," I remind him, referring to the package I received just weeks after the Dark House weekend. It was filled with the winning essays of all of my fellow contest winners. I brought the package to the authorities, but with no postmark and no fingerprints, it was another dead end.

"You're safe in here," he says, pulling his fist away. He knocks on the door, right above my head. The sound echoes off the bones of my skull.

"No!" I shout, pushing myself against him—fists and arms and chest and head.

Because he won't hear me.

Because I have to make him hear me.

Everything that happens next feels like it's been set to fast forward—like I'm watching it on a TV screen, like it isn't actually happening to me.

The door whips open and I get pushed to the side. Two nurses grab me from behind. They pull up my hospital gown, exposing my legs. Detective Thomas's eyes go straight to my knees—all bruised and swollen and purple and yellow—as a needle's stabbed into my thigh.

His face falls flat—the tension replaced by something else. Surprise? Repulsion? Pity? Remorse?

My slipper has fallen off. My heel catches against a floor tile. A layer of skin scrapes free. It takes me a moment to realize that I'm being dragged through the common room from behind.

People are talking.

Fingers are pointing.

A plastic dish falls to the floor with a clatter.

I'm brought into a room. My head hits something soft. A pillow. Cold sheets. What happened to my notebook? Where is my map?

Ticktock, ticktock. Another clock on yet another wall. But this medicine seems to do the trick, darkening my mind, dulling all of my sharp edges.

Until I can no longer hear the ticking.

Until all of my fight slips away.

NORTHBRIDGE
PSYCHIATRIC HOSPITAL

INCIDENT REPORT

Date and Time of Incident: 9/13, 3:30 p.m.

Patient Name: Ivy Rose Jensen

Age: 18

DIAGNOSIS

Post-Traumatic Stress Disorder, Depression, Anxiety
Disorder

DESCRIPTION OF INCIDENT

(as reported to Amanda Baker, C.N.P., by Detective Clive Thomas)

Detective Clive Thomas had been in Private Meeting Room
Two, per Ivy's request, to discuss details of the "Dark House"
case in which she was involved. When Detective Thomas tried
to leave the room, Ivy became hostile and began shouting at
him. (Note: the shouting was heard in the common area of
the hospital, as confirmed by Brooke Cantor, L.P.N.) Thomas
reported that Ivy took hold of the doorknob and tried to keep

him from knocking on the door. When he was finally able to knock, she shoved herself into him headfirst, and swung her arms at his face. Thomas reported that Ivy punched his jaw and elbowed his neck. At that time, nurses Dan Leiberman and Jonathan Zakum entered the room to assist.

PATIENT MEDICAL HISTORY/SHORT FORM

Adoptive Mother's Information

Name:	Gail "Apple" Jensen
Occupation:	Owner, The Tea Depot and the 24-hour Depot, Boston, MA
Marital Status:	Married

Adoptive Father's Information

Name:	Steve "Core" Jensen
Occupation:	Owner/General Contractor, Crunch Construction, Singham, MA
Marital Status:	Married

Maternal Mother's Information

Name:	Sarah Leiken
	Deceased at 41 years old
Cause of Death:	Homicide victim

Paternal Father's Information

Name: Matthew Leiken

Deceased at 44 years old

Cause of Death: Homicide victim

PATIENT'S DEVELOPMENTAL HISTORY

Past medical records for April Leiken (adoptive name, Ivy Jensen) show that April was the product of a full-term pregnancy and unremarkable birth. Neonatal is neither remarkable nor contributory, and developmental milestones for motor skills and speech/language acquisition occurred within average expectancies.

BEHAVIORAL PROBLEMS

(filled out by Gail Jensen, adoptive mother, upon hospital admittance):

Does your child currently have or has he/she ever had *(place an X beside all that apply)*:

Problems with sleeping	X
Appetite change or sudden weight change	X
Irritability or temper outbursts	X
Withdrawal or preference for being alone	X
Frequent complaints of aches or pains	(headaches) X
Recent drop in grades	N/A

(she's not currently in school)

Phobia or irrational fears	X
Difficulties separating from you	
Bouts of severe anxiety or panic	X
Repetitive behaviors (i.e., washing hands, checking locks)	X
Pulling out hair or eyelashes	(pinching) X
Talk to him/herself	
Have any imaginary friend	
Appear paranoid or afraid of others	X
Have any odd ideas or beliefs	X
Ever tried to kill themselves or others	

PAST PSYCHIATRIC HISTORY

After her maternal mother and paternal father were killed, Ivy saw Paula Laub, M.D. From the age of 9 to present, she's been seeing Donna Lamb, Ph.D.

Has your child ever been admitted to the hospital for psychiatric treatment? No.

IVY

SHE'S HERE. SITTING AT A TABLE IN THE REC ROOM, in a chair that's way too small for her. Dr. Donna looks like a little kid.

"Hi," I say, in a voice that's just as small.

She doesn't hear me. The TV's too loud. *Wheel of Fortune.* I snatch the remote from the bookcase and lower the volume. No one who's watching seems to care, or maybe they just don't notice.

"Hi," I try again, taking the seat across from her. Somehow, despite the obvious change of space—not her stuffy office but the common area of a mental hospital—I still slip into rote routine, imagining this like a rerun on TV, suddenly wishing I could click away.

IVY: Thanks for coming to see me on such short notice.

DR. DONNA: Of course. I'm always here for you, Ivy.

IVY: So, I've been thinking a lot about the case.

DR. DONNA: Have you been thinking as much about healing?

IVY: It's him.

DR. DONNA: What's him?

IVY: The man who killed my parents, the Dark House amusement park killer . . . they're one and the same.

DR. DONNA: That's one theory that the authorities are working on.

IVY: *Excuse me?*

DR. DONNA: There are a number of theories, Ivy. The authorities are doing their job by looking into all of them. They want you to do your job too—by getting rest and getter better enough to go home. Don't you want that as well?

IVY: So, they've obviously been keeping secrets from me.

DR. DONNA: Do you think that rather the authorities don't want to burden you with the details of the case as you're trying to heal?

IVY: I think they owe it to me be honest, especially when I've been telling them everything I know, everything I remember. I mean, I'm part of this investigation too, aren't I?

DR. DONNA: This might feel like an injustice right now, but it's important to put things into perspective. Your disorder can often make feelings seem exponentially bigger, stronger, and more profoundly relevant than they need to be.

IVY: This isn't about my disorder. And my feelings *are* relevant.

DR. DONNA: Of course they are. That's not what I meant.

IVY: My parents' killer was a fan of horror movies. He re-created his favorite scenes from horror flicks for his crimes—just like the Nightmare Elf killer... the way he used Justin Blake's films as his inspiration for the Dark House weekend.

DR. DONNA: Okay, but why would your parents' killer go to all the trouble of organizing the Dark House amusement park weekend, holding a contest, and involving others if he only wanted to come back for you?

IVY: Because he wanted to make his own horror movie, and he needed more than one character. He handpicked all of us contest winners for his cast.

DR. DONNA: And how would he know that you, specifically, would enter the contest... someone who hates anything even remotely fear-inducing?

IVY: He kept e-mailing me his newsletters, ignoring my attempts to unsubscribe from his supposed list. He sent me contest opportunity after contest opportunity, awaiting the day I'd finally enter one of them. I told that to Parker—how I kept getting the Nightmare Elf's newsletters—and he seemed really confused. He never knew the Nightmare Elf even had a newsletter. None of the winners did. They all found out about the contest through various fan-flavored sites—places the killer must've posted once I'd finally entered.

DR. DONNA: You've obviously given this a lot of thought.

IVY: I have a lot of time to think in here.

DR. DONNA: What's that?

IVY: What?

DR. DONNA: On your palm and wrists. Don't try to hide it, Ivy. Have you been writing on yourself?

IVY: It's just my notes. The doctor confiscated my notebook, so I have no other choice but to jot things down on my skin.

DR. DONNA: Why do you think he confiscated your notebook?

IVY: Because he's a controlling asshole.

DR. DONNA: Because he must've felt it was holding you back from getting better.

IVY: I'll be better once the killer's behind bars, once the others are found. To think the killer's been prepping me for years... sending me all those teaser gifts. The makeup kit for my theatrical performance, the star necklace pendant, because he wanted me to be his star.

DR. DONNA: And the soccer jersey and journal? Do you think that those things are related to acting and theater as well?

IVY: No, but they're just as important. They're clues that he knows who I am—before I was Ivy Jensen, that is, back when I was April Leiken, when I played soccer, and loved anything pink and covered in paisleys. Back when he killed my real parents.

DR. DONNA: Have you shared your theories with the authorities?

IVY: I'm done sharing with authorities. They've yet to help me with anything—not my parents' crime, not this one either. I need to figure things out on my own.

AUTUMN

IVY

It's six weeks later and I'm sitting in the same meeting room with the same ticking clock. But this time I'm not waiting for the police. And my palms and wrists are clean of ink. Plus my knees are no longer bruised, not that you can see them. I'm no longer dressed in a hospital gown. I'm able to wear my own clothes: my favorite sweats, my fuzzy slippers. I also got my bracelet back—six long strands of T-shirt fabric woven into a fishtail braid that winds around my wrist. The fabric is from Parker's T-shirt—the same one he wore on the Dark House amusement park night, the one he used to make a bandage for my ankle.

I touch over my heart, where my pendant used to dangle, reminded that he has something of mine too. My aromatherapy necklace. It'd fallen off as we were running to escape. One moment, we were fleeing the amusement park together, heading toward the closing exit gates. The next moment, Parker had stopped to pick something up. It took me a couple of seconds to figure out what it was.

That necklace was supposed to have been a gift for my mother. But she was killed before I could give it to her—just days before her forty-second birthday.

The necklace—a tiny bottle pendant with an even tinier cork, suspended from a silver chain—became my most cherished possession. Still, in that moment of trying to escape the park, I no longer cared about the necklace. I only cared about Parker—about him joining me on the other side of the exit gate. But time was ticking then too. The exit gates were closing. I strained my muscles, using all of the strength inside me to hold the doors open. But in the end, the iron gates closed with a deep, heavy clank, locking Parker inside the park.

And tearing my world in two.

At last, the door to the conference room opens and I sit up straighter. I smile—not too big, a closed mouth—and make direct eye contact as Dr. Tully comes in. He's older, mid-sixties, with hair like Albert Einstein and the tiniest glasses I've ever seen. He's the bigwig here. Patients don't normally meet with him, except upon admission or when there's a serious problem.

Or just prior to exit.

He starts with small talk, asking me a few basic questions— about the weather and the food here, and if I noticed the full moon last night. I haven't missed a week of therapy for the past seven years, so I know just how to answer, lying straight through my teeth.

"I love the winter," I tell him. "My foster parents rent a place in Vermont and we go up on the weekends to ski. I can't wait to get back there." The truth: I've never been skiing. But my answer shows that I'm looking ahead, excited about life, not intimidated by the thought of spending time with family.

"The food here?" I flash him a sheepish grin. "Well, it's not exactly fine dining, especially for a food snob like me who wants to be a chef. Although, between you and me"—I lean in close— "the mac and cheese here kicks my recipe's butt." The lie nearly kills me, but the outcome is totally worth it.

Dr. Tully grins at my answer. I've shown him my sense of humor while, at the same time, conveying my aspirations.

And as for that magnificent moon: "Yes, I saw it. It was so big and glowing, like a giant snowball in the sky."

It's true that I noticed the moon. I'd have to have been an idiot not to, considering that a couple of the patients were howling at it. But it didn't make me think of a snowball. It made me think of Parker—made me wonder if, wherever he is, he could see it too.

The remainder of the interview is key, because he segues into the reason that I'm here: "How often do you think about the Dark House amusement park night?"

I swallow hard, trying to keep a poker face. The truth is that I don't remember what it was like to *not* think about that night. "I don't know," I answer, finally. "At least once a day. I no longer dream about it, though; and it's not the first thing on my mind when I wake up in the morning. I'm hoping that with more time—and closure—I won't think about it much at all." Breathe in, breathe out. *Ticktock, ticktock.* I keep my hands on the table, where both he and I can see them, resisting the urge to pinch.

"And what if you don't get that closure?" he asks. "What if the others aren't found and they never catch the person responsible?"

"I've been working on my own form of closure, trying to think up things I can do, ways I can help people, maybe talking to crisis victims . . . people who've had loved ones taken away from them. I don't know." I feign a shy smile. "Does that sound dumb?"

Dr. Tully leans forward. A good sign; my answer has piqued his interest. "It actually sounds very ambitious."

"I realize that. And I know I have a lot more healing to do before I can help others. But it's definitely in my long-term plans."

"Well, I think it's a great plan." He smiles, perhaps relieved by my newfound sanity and perspective—all thanks to Happy Hospital. "You've been through a lot in your lifetime—more tragedy than most people will ever know. It's healthy to think of that tragedy as a springboard to do good. Talk about your notebook, and your maps and charts. Are you still writing down all of your theories and trying to track the person responsible for the Dark House weekend?"

I shake my head, glad that he asked. "I threw all of that stuff away—not long after the doctor confiscated my notebook, actually. It was feeding an obsession and keeping me from moving forward. I can see that now."

"Do you still feel the need to help solve the case and find the missing victims?"

I shake my head again. "That isn't up to me. The FBI know what they're doing. My job is to get better and to get out of here." The very same words that Detective Thomas used on me.

"Well, you've certainly come a long way." He eyes me for several seconds, studying my body language and nodding his head.

Meanwhile, I do my best not to swallow too hard or blink too often.

"I'd like to talk to you about the hospital's outpatient program," he says, finally. "It's important that you continue your therapy upon discharge."

I hold in my elation by squeezing my thighs together. "I'd like that."

"You'll be responsible for taking all of your medication. And should you ever feel overwhelmed, or overly stressed, or excessively anxious or fearful about anything, it's essential that you tell someone. Before your discharge, we'll establish a list of go-to people to call. How does that sound?"

"It sounds perfect." I flash him another closed smile.

In my room, I celebrate my get-out-of-jail card by packing up my stuff. While my roommate is at her group session, I move to the far wall by my dresser. I peek over my shoulder to make sure no one's looking in from the hallway, and then I scoot down by the heat vent and take off the cover. My notebook—a new one—is stuffed inside the duct. I snag it, replace the cover, and flip the notebook open to the back—to a letter I'm writing to Parker. The pages warm me like a blanket.

Dear Parker,

My mind reels, going over the details of the Dark House weekend, trying to come up with an answer—some unturned leaf, a magical pearl that might help to find you and the others.

Questions I wish I could ask you: Are you okay? The obvious: Where are you? Who's with you? Frankie, Shayla, Garth, Natalie? Will you ever forgive me for leaving you at the park?

Things I wish I could tell you: I miss you more than you know. I'll never stop looking for you.

Love always,

Ivy

IVY

IT'S BEEN NEARLY FIVE WEEKS SINCE MY RELEASE from the hospital, and a lot of things have changed. For starters, I didn't go home to my foster parents. I moved into the basement apartment of Tillie, my foster aunt, just down the street. It's better this way. More privacy for me. Less potential danger for them.

For my entire life, no one around me has ever been safe.

"Aunt Tillie has a security system," Apple reminded me, zipping up my suitcase.

Without any of my things, my room looked like it belonged in a hotel—like a place that one might inhabit for a limited amount of time, which, I suppose, is exactly what I did.

"This will always be your home," Core insisted, standing in the doorway.

I thanked them, hugged them, and told them I felt the same way. But, all the while, I couldn't help but feel an overwhelming sense of relief. Things would be easier on my own.

Another thing that's changed: I'm working now, full-time at the 24-Hour Depot, Apple's new restaurant in the center of town. I never did end up going to Paris for culinary school, as I'd been planning for the past three years.

I'm at the Depot right now, working the overnight shift, since it's not like I get any sleep anyway. One thing this job has taught me: I'm not alone in my insomnia. We have dozens of regulars who frequent this place, seeking camaraderie in their sleeplessness and solitude.

I pick up my knife, feeling an instant jolt of power, relishing the fit of the handle inside my grip. Using a soup bowl as a guide, I point the tip of the blade into a rolled-out sheet of dough and cut out a series of disks.

Gretchen, the hostess, pokes her head through the pass-through window, nearly knocking over a plate full of chicken-fried pickles. "Just a little FYI: there's a heaping hunk of hotness sitting at table eleven."

"I'm busy," I say, eyeing the trays full of pastry dough that I still need to cut.

"Suit yourself." She pops a pickle into her mouth. "Just trying to keep you in the know. Isn't that what you said you wanted? Candy and I have dubbed him the sexy squatter, by the way, because he's been nursing a cherry Coke and cheese fries for the past two hours."

I look up from my slicing. "Did you ask him if he wanted anything else?"

"Well, of course, I'm not an amateur." She rolls her big blue eyes. "But he says he's happy just sitting."

"Is he working on a laptop? Or waiting for someone?"

"No. And no. I already asked about that latter one."

"And you're sure it's been two hours?" *Ticktock, ticktock.*

She nods and pops another pickle.

The knife still gripped in my hand, I dart out of the kitchen. The dining area is sprinkled with customers—a mixture of regulars, some newbies, and a gaggle of college students pigging out after a party. "Where?"

"There." Gretchen nods.

Sitting at the corner booth with his back facing us, Mr. Mystery has slick dark hair and a leather jacket.

"A pretty fine specimen, wouldn't you say? And that's just from behind. Wait till you get the full-frontal view." She gives

of hello. He closes the door and sits down across from me with a notepad and pen.

"She called me," I tell him. "Just now. She asked if I was coming for them."

"Okay, hold on, *who* called you?"

"Natalie." Didn't I mention that?

"How do you know it was her?"

"It was a private call, but it sounded like her."

He doesn't write anything down. "Did this person say anything else?"

"It was *her*," I insist. "Don't you think we should do something—tell someone?" *Why is it so hot in here?* I look around for a heat vent.

"How long did the conversation last?"

"A few seconds."

"A few seconds isn't exactly long enough to prove anything."

I know. It isn't. *Ticktock, ticktock.* I clench my teeth, feeling my skin begin to itch.

"There's more."

"Okay." His forehead furrows.

"There was a guy at the diner during my shift."

"And?"

"And he called me *Princess*," I say, proceeding to tell him how the guy had been hanging around the diner for more than two hours, and how it seemed he might've been waiting for me. "I'm pretty sure he was in his twenties. He had dark hair, hazel eyes, and he drove a Ford pick—"

"*And?*" Thomas asks again.

"What do you mean *and*?" I balk. "He called me *Princess* ... just like I wrote about in my nightmare essay for the contest, just like the Nightmare Elf called me when he re-created my nightmare. Do you really think it's a coincidence?"

"I don't know. It could be."

"Would *you* call a complete stranger a princess?"

"Maybe if I were a twenty-something-year-old guy looking to flirt with a girl."

"It wasn't a coincidence. It was a warning. The killer's coming back for me again. He wants me to be in his next movie."

"We're not even sure there was a first movie—at least there wasn't one discovered."

"It exists," I snap. "I saw it. I lived it. The Nightmare Elf made us watch it." Our experience during the Dark House weekend was recorded; the killer was using that footage to make a feature film.

"Let's just say that this guy at the diner...his calling you a princess wasn't a coincidence.... Maybe he found your essay online."

"It isn't online," I say, thinking how I wondered the same—how I asked the mystery boy if he'd found my essay on some site.

"Not that you know of." Thomas gives me a pointed look. "Maybe he's some die-hard Justin Blake fan, wanting to meet the girl who got away."

"Or maybe he came as a messenger," I say, "from the killer himself."

"Did he say anything else that might link him to the case?"

I shake my head and look away, almost tempted to make something up.

"Well, you don't need *me* to tell you that people are interested in your story, Ivy. In some way, you've become famous. A lot of Justin Blake fans would go to great lengths—including frequenting your place of employment—to meet you. To them, you're a real-life heroine."

"I'm hardly a heroine." Heroes don't leave others behind.

"Sounds like someone's being too hard on herself. Are you still taking care of yourself, getting the help you need?"

"If you're talking about outpatient therapy, then the answer is yes," I lie, knowing he has a point about the story's appeal. After the Dark House weekend, varied versions of the story spiraled out of control. Hard-core Justin Blake fans created videos depicting their own ideas of what happened. They posted them online, some even insisting that their films were the real deal. Last time I checked, there were more than two hundred phony films.

Also after that weekend, I started receiving prank phone calls (people claiming to be Natalie, Parker, and the others), as well as lame-o invitations and admission tickets to see the screening of numerous Nightmare Elf–inspired projects.

"Why isn't the FBI looking harder?" I ask him.

"They *are* looking hard. This *is* a serious case. We have five missing people and a potential killer on the loose. In my book, that's top priority."

"And in the FBI's book?"

"Would it make you feel any better if I had an undercover detective frequent your place of work? I already have cops staked out at your parents' and aunt's residences."

"It would make me feel better if we were on the same page—if you let me in on the investigation. I shouldn't have to hear from my therapist that my real parents' killer is a suspect."

"No one's excluding you, Ivy. We're just looking out for your best interest, as well as the best interest of the case."

"It's in my best interest to find the killer and find the others."

Detective Thomas studies my face for several moments, tapping his pencil against the pad, as if calculating his next few words. "Does the name Houdini mean anything to you?"

"Houdini, as in the magician?"

"As in the serial killer. He hasn't been active for a few years now. His crimes typically involve a magic-show theme. Like the Nightmare Elf suspect, he wears a costume and creates elaborate setups using lights, props, theater staging, video equipment. After he kills his victims, he moves the bodies; they don't turn up until months later, and when they do, it's in some showy, magical fashion."

"And the Feds think that he's the same person who organized the Dark House weekend? Do they have a concrete reason? Fingerprints? DNA?"

"It's just one of the many theories right now."

"In other words, no."

"We can't dismiss theories based on lack of evidence."

"Maybe you should take your own advice."

"*Excuse me?*"

"The Nightmare Elf's theme is horror, not magic," I remind him.

"Still, there are enough common threads to raise suspicion, especially since Houdini's victims fit the profile of your group: an eclectic mix of college-age students looking for a good time. The victims are often tricked into going to see a magic show; there's usually some element of winning a contest."

"What if the Nightmare Elf killer knew about Houdini and was trying to copy his style? What if he was hoping that you'd pin the Dark House weekend crimes on Houdini?"

"Ivy..."

"*What?*" I ask, able to hear the ticktock deep inside me. It throbs against my chest, echoing inside my brain. "You're wasting your time on any other theory that doesn't involve my real parents' killer."

"I've said it once and I'll say it again: leave the manhunt to the experts, okay?" He closes his notepad and tucks it inside his jacket.

"What about Taylor?" I persist.

"The FBI already spoke to her."

"So how come I haven't heard the outcome? Why did she leave the Dark House early?"

Taylor was supposed to have been my roommate for that weekend. She and Natalie were the first to arrive at the house. But not long after their arrival, Taylor left, in the midst of unpacking—without her bags, without her cell phone, without a word to Natalie that she was leaving. Later, we found a message in Taylor's closet, scrawled against the back wall: GET OUT BEFORE IT'S TOO LATE. I'm pretty sure Taylor wrote it—pretty confident that it was her way of trying to warn us.

"I need to talk to Taylor," I tell him. "We need to compare notes, fill in blanks, discuss each other's chronology...."

"Whatever Taylor claims to have seen at the Dark House is of no concern to you right now."

"Can you arrange for the two of us to meet?"

Thomas leans forward, as if about to let me in on a secret. "You're what, three weeks out of a mental hospital?"

"Five weeks." I swallow hard.

"And how many times have you called and/or come to see me since then?"

"Four?"

"Try fourteen," he says, his voice softening. "Fourteen times in five weeks. Now, I know this must be frustrating, and it's not that I don't appreciate your input, but my advice for you?"

"Forget it," I say, getting up from the table. I go for the door, slamming it shut behind me.

TAYLOR MONROE

DOZENS OF DANCE RECITAL DRESSES HOVER ABOVE MY *head. The tassels dangle into my eyes. The unsettled dust makes me have to sneeze. But I can't. I won't. I have to remain still.*

I'm hiding inside a closet, tucked behind the dancing bear costume from The Nutcracker Suite.

Someone comes into the room. I hear a floorboard creak. The sound of feet scuff against the carpeted floor. There's a sniffle and then a cough. Did someone open a dresser drawer? Is that my suitcase being zipped?

"I don't think she's in here." Midge's voice. "No, I already searched

it," she says, talking on the phone. "Yes, of course. That one's already done too. Are you even listening to me? I think she might've left."

The closet door slides open. The costumes shift forward and back. I'm at the far end, against the wall, about to lose my lunch. My hand is bleeding. The wound is throbbing.

"Wait a second," Midge says, still talking on the phone.

The costumes push forward again. Sequins poke into my eye.

"Come on, now. You aren't really implying what I think you are, are you?" she continues. "Well, then you can go to hell."

The phone beeps a couple of seconds later. I think she hung up mid-conversation. I hear the door shut.

My heart pounding, I grab the lip-gloss tube that's in my pocket and write the word KILLER across the wall.

"Taylor?"

I write KILLER again, bearing down so hard that the tube snaps in half. Blood from my hand spurts over the rug.

"Earth to Taylor Monroe," someone sings.

And that's when I realize . . . when I snap out of my daydream.

I look down at my notebook. The word KILLER is scrawled across the page. My pencil—not my lip gloss—has snapped in two. There is no blood; the cut on my hand has long since healed.

Chantel I-never-stop-playing-with-my-hair Coughlin, my resident advisor, is standing over me, twirling a curlicue around her finger. We're in the dorm lobby. At school. There are groups of students sprinkled about the space—doing their homework, sipping their coffee, texting on phones, and chatting among themselves.

"Holy embarrassing moment, Batgirl." My face fries with heat. I close up my notebook.

Chantel flashes me a polite smile, as if my nutty behavior is totally normal and doesn't warrant a snarky comment.

"I totally zoned out, didn't I?" I've been doing that lately, having flashbacks, getting cold sweats, murmuring to myself like some *Twilight Zone*–ish freak. "Lack of sleep does some funky stuff to people, doesn't it?" I fake a giggle.

"I have some good news," she says, straight-faced, all business, still curl-twirling. "It took some doing, but we were able to move your case to the top of our priority list."

"I have a case?" I ask, feeling the confusion on my face.

"A single room will be opening up sooner than anticipated. We should be able to get you in by the end of next week."

"Couldn't I just switch roommates?" I ask, pretty sure that I sound like a broken record. "It'll be kind of weird living alone. I mean, I came here to be with people."

"You'll love having your own room," Chantel says, bringing a strand of hair up to her lips for a taste. "You won't have to worry about a roommate talking your ear off while you're trying to study, or having her friends barge in at all hours of the day and night while you're trying to get work done, or—the worst—eating all of your food."

"I practically have my own room *now*," I say, referring to Emily's absence. "And I absolutely hate it."

Emily and I were assigned as roommates, only she moved out (to crash on her BFF Barbie's spare futon) after only a few weeks into the semester, telling everyone that she couldn't possibly be expected to sleep in the same room as a killer.

"Plus, all of that barging-in-and-eating-each-other's-food stuff…" I continue. "It actually sounds pretty nice."

"You'll love it," she insists, voiding out my words with a jingle of her dollar-store bracelets; there are at least twenty silver bangles loaded on her arm. She lets them slide up and down her wrist as she talks—her own sort of background noise.

"Aren't there any other options?" I ask. "Somebody else who needs to switch roommates? I'd be happy to meet with them first. I mean, seriously." I feel my eyes begin to fill. "I'm not as horrible as everybody thinks. I was voted Most Popular in high school for three years in a row, for God's sake." My words sound stupid and desperate, and that's exactly what they are.

Chantel continues to stare at me, a plastic smile on her face, as if none of what I'm saying matters. *Jingle, jangle, jingle.* A second later, my own background noise kicks in: My phone rings in my pocket. I don't recognize the number.

"Go ahead and take it," Chantel says, as I'm about to hit IGNORE. "I have to run. I just wanted to let you know that everything is all set."

I try my best to hold it together as Chantel turns on her heel, joining a group of sorority pledges in the corner of the lobby (all dressed up like Elvis), leaving me without a say.

My phone continues to ring. I click on it to answer, eager for some love, even if it's in the shape of some nonexistent prize I need to claim: "Hello?"

"Taylor?"

"Yes."

"This is Ivy Jensen. We spoke on the phone once before... when I was at the amusement park... during the Dark House weekend."

"Wait, how did you get my number?"

"It was attached to your contest essay. It's sort of a long story, but the essays showed up in my mailbox one day. I really think we should talk."

"Okay, but I've already told the police everything I know."

"I realize that, but I was hoping that if we got together and compared notes, we could come up with some new ideas."

"Ideas for what? The FBI already has our testimonies."

"Well, I think that we can do better than the FBI."

The conversation falls silent. I don't know what to say, except that I don't want to talk about the Dark House anymore—about why I left, or what I saw, or what I could've done differently.

"*Taylor?*"

"We're not the police."

"Can we just meet and talk?"

I gaze out at the lobby of students. The group of sorority pledges attempts to serenade all of us by singing "Hound Dog" by Elvis, only it sounds more like *hedgehog*, which is so completely distracting.

"I'm really sorry, Ivy. But I've got a lot on my plate right now, and I need to stay focused on my studies."

"But people are still missing," she says.

"Okay, but aren't those people believed to be dead?"

"Do *you* believe it?"

"I don't have any reason not to. I mean, it's been more than three months, and there was so much blood everywhere."

"How about this reason: If you went missing but your body had yet to be uncovered, would you want people to stop looking ... to just assume that you were dead?"

"I'm really sorry," I tell her again, still focused on the sorority girls and wishing that I were one of them. If this were before the Dark House weekend, there's no doubt in my mind that I would be.

"Can we at least talk on the phone, sometime when you have more ti—"

"I'm sorry," I say, cutting her off. "I just can't do this right now." I hang up before she can argue. And then I go back to my room and cry myself to sleep.

headband, which coordinates with her pink and paisley wristlet. Way too tacky, but that can't possibly be what's got Ivy all upset.

A few seconds later, the movie fades to black and Ivy stands up. She's trembling. Her face is white. She looks like she's about to hurl. "It's him," she whispers.

"Whoa, wait, what's him?"

"I told them. I knew it." She turns away, headed for the door.

"Ivy—wait," I call.

She doesn't listen. She doesn't answer me. She simply grabs her bag and goes for the door.

Ivy

I RUN.

I run faster than I've ever run before—as far as my legs will take me. Down a stairwell, through the lobby, across a parking lot, past a soccer field, and up at least a hundred tiny steps.

Standing by a giant clock tower, I try to catch my breath, my lungs straining, my heart aching. A cold breeze brushes against my neck, sends chills down my spine.

The campus is sprawled out beneath me. The lights are on in several of the buildings, and yet everything appears vacant.

"Ivy?"

I turn to look.

It's Taylor. She comes and stands beside me, wipes my tears with the sleeve of her sweatshirt, and then wraps her arms around my shoulders. She smells like maple syrup. "It's going to be okay," she tells me. "You're safe here."

If only that were true. But things are not okay. And I'm not safe anywhere—not while the killer's still out there, studying me, directing my every move. He knew that I'd eventually reach out to Taylor, and that we'd compare videos, just like he knew how to get me to enter the Nightmare Elf's contest last year.

Taylor pulls me closer, and I rest my head against her shoulder. I can't stop shaking. My mind won't stop reeling. Why can't I remember what Mom, Dad, and I had been talking about at the diner that day? Or the reason that Dad laughed? Or what Mom said in response. The fact that I can't remember those things widens the hole in my heart.

"The campus is pretty at night, isn't it?" Taylor asks. "All lit up. Sometimes when I feel like running away, I'll come here and remind myself how lucky I am."

"Lucky because you got away?"

"Lucky for a lot of things, I guess."

"I wish I felt lucky too, but sometimes I wish that I'd died right along with them."

She pulls away to look into my face. "Don't talk like that. I mean, I know this'll probably sound majorly cliché, but you have your whole life in front of you. Plus, it's like you said before: maybe the others are still alive."

"I was talking about my parents. Sometimes I wish that I'd died right along with them seven years ago."

Her expression shows no surprise; she must've heard that my parents were murdered.

"I'm going to find the killer," I tell her.

"Wait." Her eyes slam shut. "Your parents' killer? Or the Nightmare Elf killer?"

"They're one and the same."

"Excuse me?"

"The person who organized the Dark House weekend is the same person that killed my parents. No one can deny it anymore."

Taylor makes a confused face—her lip snarled, her nose scrunched.

"I'm going to find him," I say again. *Ticktock, ticktock.* The ticking of the clock tower vibrates inside my chest. Only instead of rattling my bones, it's somewhat motivating, reminding me that time is of the essence and I have so much work to do.

IVY

BACK IN TAYLOR'S ROOM, WE SIT IN FRONT OF THE computer. The video is paused. The air feels stifling. There's a twisting sensation in my gut.

"That's me," I say, nodding toward the screen.

"Hold on, *what's* you?"

"The girl on the screen, at the diner. That was me," I attempt to explain. "Seven years ago. Those were my parents—the ones who were murdered."

"Wait, *what*?"

"I know it sounds crazy, bu—"

"Are you sure?" She fast-forwards to a spot where the camera zooms in on me—where I'm resting my head on Mom's shoulder. My face looks a lot thinner now. My cheekbones are sharper. My chin is more pointed. My hair is darker, straighter, longer. But still, my eyes are unmistakable—light brown, slightly angled, with somewhat droopy lids.

"Holy shit," Taylor says, looking back at me, studying my face.

"I remember the day this video was taken," I tell her. "I'd gone to a diner with my parents and we'd sat at that checkerboard table. I remember playing checkers with the jam and peanut butter containers. My parents were murdered just a couple of days later."

"Holy shit," she says again. "We need to show this to the police. I mean, do you seriously get what this means?"

"That the killer's been watching me for years."

"Exactly, which is, like, *crazy town.*"

"It may be crazy, but it's also what I've suspected all along. Even before the Dark House weekend, I'd be walking home from school or shopping in town somewhere and feel his eyes on me."

"And you didn't tell anyone?"

"Of course I told. My therapist knew. She thought I was being paranoid. She still does."

"Okay, so if this crazed killer has been watching you for years—and wants you to know it—why would he send the link to *me*? Why not send it to you? I mean, to me it's pretty meaningless."

"Because he wanted us to meet. And he was willing to wait until we did—until the two of us got together and compared notes."

"But what if instead of sharing the link with you, I showed it to the police?"

"You didn't have time to show them, though, did you? Didn't you say you got this link just before I got here?"

"Minutes before." She nods.

I replay the video again, searching for a clue—some hidden message as to where the others might be. Unlike the video of Natalie, this one wasn't uploaded by Movie Marvin. It was posted to Filmeo, a site where filmmakers showcase their works-in-progress—only this one hasn't been made public. Words sit at the top of the screen: EXCLUSIVE VIEWING PERMISSION.

"He posted this just for us," I whisper, proceeding to fill her in about the video of Natalie.

"And so obviously the videos were made by two different people," she says.

"Not obviously. The e-mail address is the same. The Nightmare Elf at Gmail."

"Are you sure?"

I nod. "In the video of Natalie, she was wearing a gold bracelet with a star charm . . . just like the necklace pendant I received years ago."

"Wait, what pendant?"

"I've gotten a number of anonymous gifts," I explain, "ever since my parents' death." I click on the Nightmare Elf's Filmeo account. There's no other information listed about him, or any other videos posted. I click on the link to e-mail him. A form pops up, asking for my name and e-mail address.

"You're not seriously going to send him a message, are you?"

"If the person who posted this video isn't the real killer, he's at least had contact with him."

"Ivy."

"What?" I turn to face her again.

She's looking at me like I'm a full-on freak, her eyes bulging, her lips parted like there's something hairy in her mouth. "We have to show this to the police."

I ignore her and continue to type.

Dear Nightmare Elf,

If this is really you, what did I put on my plate on that first night at the Dark House, when all of the winners were gathered at the dining room table for dinner?

Yours truly,

Ivy Jensen

P.S. If you wanted to come back for me so badly, why did you wait so long?

I read the message over several times, thinking how silly that first part sounds, but also confident that it will answer my question. No one besides the killer, Midge, and the other contest winners would know what I put my plate; I didn't get that specific in my police statement.

I position my cursor over the SEND tab, my heart absolutely racing. And then I hit SEND.

"I can't even believe you just did that," Taylor says. "Did you e-mail Movie Marvin too?"

"I did, but I didn't get any response." Not from any of my e-mail accounts, not even when I posed as an indie filmmaker looking to have a trailer made. "I'm thinking it's because I showed that video to the police."

"We have to show *this* to the police," she says yet again. "I mean, we're talking about a major piece of evidence."

I clench my teeth and look away.

"Ivy? Okay, you're acting a little *One Flew Over the Cuckoo's Nest*—and not in a good way." She stares at my balled-up fists.

I take a deep breath, my adrenaline pumping. But somehow I also feel calmer than I have in months, more confident than ever before. "I can't go to the police," I say. "The killer wants me to do this on my own."

"Well, um, *duh*. Of course he does—so he can chop you up into a million pieces and throw you into a sinkhole."

"I've given the police seven years," I tell her, "and what have they done for me so far? My parents are dead. Five people are missing and assumed dead, including a boy I really care about—the first person I've opened up to since my parents' death. What more could the killer possibly take from me?"

"Only your life."

I focus on the video again. It's paused at a close-up of my eyes, back when there was a spark in them—when I laughed, and had friends, and looked forward to tomorrow. "I've spent the majority of my life feeling dead, fearing death, or wishing I had died."

"This isn't a game, Ivy."

"It is to him. And he wants to play. But this time I refuse to lose."

"Okay, seriously? It's time for some tough love. Let's push the pause on the intensity button, shall we? We need to think things through."

"I'm intense for good reason."

"Okay, but too much intensity and people wind up storing chicken carcasses under their beds. Didn't you see *Girl, Interrupted*? What you need is some Handyman Harry." She holds up a keychain doll: a bearded little guy wearing blue-jean overalls and work boots. She presses his gut to make him talk.

"Hey there, hottie," Handyman Harry says. "Do you want to see my big screwdriver?"

126

"What do you think you're doing?"

"Not what, *who*." She winks. "I won him during freshman orientation for having the loudest belch. The loudest boy belcher got Harry's sister, Handygal Harriet." Taylor follows up with a burrito-and-soda-worthy belch so loud that it almost sounds fake. "Pretty impressive, wouldn't you say?" Taylor continues to press the doll's belly.

A series of terrible pickup lines play out of Harry's mouth: "Hey, baby, how about we build a future together? We can start with my hammer and some nailing"; "Hey, angel, does your crack need some caulking?"; "Do your shrubs need pruning?"

Taylor pretends to make out with the doll—*with* tongue—finally shoving it down the front of her sweatshirt. "Oh, Handyman Harry!" she purrs, tossing and turning on the bed, her eyes rolled back, her body quivering.

I can't help but laugh, even though I don't want to. And the harder I try to stop it, the stronger my giggles get. My stomach aches as tears streak down my face. Ironically, this is the worst time of my life and yet I haven't laughed as hard in years.

From the Journal of E.W.
Grade 7, August Preparatory School

LATE AUTUMN 1971

I just found out that some kid who used to go here killed himself. His name was Ricky Slater, and I've been assigned to his old room. Tray across the hall says that I'm the first person to sleep in Ricky's room since the suicide. He said that the room had been closed off for painting and refinishing, as if that would make everything nice. Too bad it doesn't work that way.

Gramps once bought Mother a pretty yellow sundress, but that didn't change squat. That same night she crawled into my bed and told me a ghost story—about a twelve-year-old boy named Johnny who'd lived on our property a hundred years ago, and died when the house went up in flames.

"Johnny was an angry, angry boy because of it." I can still hear Mother's little-girl voice.

I was six years old, and couldn't sleep after that. When Mother saw how scared I got with Johnny's story, she made a habit of visiting my room each night with a different, more horrifying tale about him.

"He may have died that day," she'd say, "but he's still here, in this house. Ever feel someone's eyes on you when you're in the bathtub or reading a book? That's him. That's Johnny, watching, studying, learning all of your habits. He talks to me, you know. He tells me how angry he still is and what I could do to make him feel better."

I'd beg her to stop talking about him. Sometimes I'd even pretend to be asleep. But it didn't matter. She was there, every night, whispering in my ear, waiting for me to cry. Only then would she leave me alone, which in some way was even worse, because I'd look around my room—at my stuffed lion and the nutcracker doll on my desk—and think they were possessed by Johnny's spirit.

People are saying that this school is haunted by the ghost of Ricky Slater. I wonder if Nana and Gramps knew that when they signed me up, and if they might've even requested that I get Ricky's room.

I'll bet anything they did. They knew about my mother's nightly ghost stories, but they didn't do crap to stop them.

IVY

EVEN THOUGH I GOT A HOTEL ROOM, TAYLOR INSISTS that I stay in her dorm.

"Let's just sleep on stuff, okay?" She opens up the futon and dresses it in pear-patterned sheets. "We won't make any major decisions until after we get some shut-eye. Oh, and P.S. sorry if the cushions smell like pickles. Sometimes I get a craving, and one time I spilled a jar."

We wash up and get changed—me in sweats and her in lipstick-kiss-patterned footie pajamas—and then crawl into our beds. It's just after one in the morning, but instead of going off to sleep,

Taylor rolls over to face me. "I'm really glad we did this—that you called me, that I called you back, that you came here."

"Because I'm so much fun to be with, right?"

"More fun than I've had in weeks, to be honest. Sad but true. I mean, no offense."

"None taken."

"And now inquiring minds want to know: Do you blame me too?"

"*Blame you?*"

"For leaving the Dark House. For not taking Natalie with me, for not hiding somewhere—in the woods, maybe—and trying to warn you guys as you arrived."

"A lot of people would've done the same," I tell her. "Escaped from the Dark House, that is."

"Would *you* have done the same?"

I bite my lip, thinking back to how scared I was that weekend. "Part of me thinks that even if I'd wanted to bolt, I never would've made it out of there. I would've been paralyzed by my fear."

"By the time Natalie even crossed my mind, I was already deep into the woods. That message I wrote in the closet—get out before it's too late—just tells you how much of a coward I was. It was done on a whim, while I was hiding from Midge. I'm surprised you even found it."

"But I *did* find it. And I never forgot it. I knew something about it wasn't right."

Taylor shrugs. "I should've done so much more."

"You did the best you could at the time," I say, channeling my inner Dr. Donna.

"It was a full day and a half before I was able to get help," she says. "After I escaped, I still wasn't in the clear; someone was chasing me in the woods."

"Did you see who that someone was?"

"No, but eventually, when I got far enough away, I hid behind a fallen tree, my cheek pressed against a sharp twig, trying not to move. I stayed like that for hours, exactly as you describe— paralyzed by fear. I didn't move again until daylight."

"On Saturday," I say to be sure. "The day we went to the amusement park."

"Exactly." She nods. "It took a long time to find the road, and even longer to get picked up. But I did. A couple of truckers found me. They didn't speak English. Neither of them had a phone. And I didn't want to risk having them stop their truck. I just wanted to get away. They brought me to a bus depot and paid for my ticket. I ended up in Minneapolis, where I called the police. But I didn't know where the Dark House was—not really. And I just kept thinking about all of you guys, wondering what was happening."

She looks away, her eyes filled with tears. "It seems like all I've been doing lately is wondering *what if.*"

"But hindsight is twenty-twenty, right?"

"So you don't hate me?"

I get up from the bed to bring her a box of tissues. "Of course not. Far from it."

"Well, that's a relief, because I was so afraid to meet you."

I sit down beside her and blot her tears with a tissue. "Well, I'm really glad that we *did* meet—that you changed your mind about getting together." Because this is the closest I've felt to anyone since Parker. And it feels good to be the strong one for a change—even if it's just in this moment.

Ivy

I WAKE UP TO A BUZZING SOUND. MY CELL PHONE vibrates against the floor. I have a new e-mail message.

I sit up in bed. It's three a.m. Taylor's still asleep. A smiley face sleep mask covers her eyes; the front of it reads HAPPY NAPPER.

I reach for my phone to check who the message is from. The brightness of the screen stings my eyes and I have to squint.

But still I can see it: the Nightmare Elf's name in my in-box.

My heart tightens. The phone slips from my grip, clanking to the floor, waking Taylor up.

She pulls down her sleep mask. "What is it?"

"He wrote me back."

She sits up, clicks on her night table light, and then comes to join me on the futon.

The e-mail's subject line reads TO ANSWER YOUR QUESTIONS. I click to read the message.

Dearest Ivy,

How nice to hear from you. I trust this finds you well.

To answer your first question, you didn't really put too much on your dinner plate on the night of your Dark House arrival, despite the feast that had been arranged—the very same meal served in *Nightmare Elf III: Lights Out.* The smallest mound of macaroni and cheese was all.

Your other question intrigues me, but I think I'll answer it at another time.

—The Nightmare Elf

I clasp my hand over my mouth, feeling my entire body shake.

"Is that true?" Taylor asks. "About the mac and cheese?"

"True." I nod. There's a sharpness in my chest, making it hard to breathe.

Taylor gets up to grab her laptop off her desk. Meanwhile, I reach into my bag for a sachet of lemon balm. I hold it up to my nose, concentrating on its ability to soothe.

"What the hell?" she shouts, sitting beside me again.

There's an error message on the computer screen. Taylor tries refreshing the page—it's the Filmeo account; I can tell from the URL. But the video's gone. The account appears to have been deleted.

"What happened?" she asks. She goes back to the original e-mail message, copies the link, and then pastes it into the browser. But the error message is still there. "We should call the police. They might be able to trace the e-mail address—or the server, that is—to find out where this person's located."

"I'm assuming they're already doing that. I mean, they have the e-mail address from the Movie Marvin video." The police tried tracing the original Nightmare Elf e-mails from a year ago as well, only, for whatever reason, they weren't able to pinpoint a location.

"Let's just go talk to them." She gets up and returns to her bed, closing the laptop.

My phone vibrates again. It's another message from the Nightmare Elf. The subject line reads: RAIN, RAIN, GO AWAY.

I click to open it up. The words *Do you like a wet seat?* make my head spin.

"What is it?" Taylor asks.

I look up in her direction, but then my eyes fix on the window behind her. Rain pounds against the glass.

"*What?*" she persists.

I get up and bolt out the door.

TAYLOR

IVY RUNS FROM MY ROOM—YET AGAIN. I FOLLOW HER
out—down the stairs and through the lobby—calling after her in
my loudest whisper to avoid waking anyone up.

I push through the exit doors. Ivy is a good distance in front
of me. There are streetlamps shining over the parking lot, but it's
still hard to see. It's raining out. The droplets pelt my eyes, making me wish I had my sleep mask, or at least an umbrella.

Ivy moves like a contestant on *Supermarket Dash*, weaving
through cars (in lieu of store displays), trying to find her own car
(instead of a prize-winning box of Cheerios).

"Ivy?" I call, once again.

She stops in front of a small dark sedan a couple of rows over. I hurry closer, able to see that the windows of the car are open.

She swings open the driver's side door and reaches inside to retrieve something from the seat.

"What is it?" I ask, standing right behind her now.

"My windows weren't open," she mumbles.

"Well, I should hope not. This isn't exactly Punta Cana. I'm freezing my ass cheeks off."

She snags a flashlight from her glove box and shines it over a bright red envelope. The front of it reads FOR APRIL, WITH LOVE, in black block lettering. "He's here," she whispers; there's a tremor in her voice.

I take the umbrella sticking out from the side door compartment. I open it up and hold it over us. Meanwhile, Ivy aims her flashlight all around—over cars, at windshields—before going to tear the envelope open.

"Hold up," I say, stopping her a moment by grabbing her wrist. "This is tangible evidence. We shouldn't even touch it. We should just bring it to the police."

She ignores me and continues to rip it open, her dampened fingers unable to work fast enough. Finally, she pulls out a card. "An invitation."

"To where?"

She reads it over, her jaw clenched, her nostrils flared.

"What does it say?" I ask.

She turns it over so I can see.

YOU'VE BEEN CHOSEN ONCE AGAIN

What: To claim your leading role as the star of *Return to the Dark House.*

Where: On set, at an undisclosed location.

When: Filming begins as soon as you're ready to commit to the project.

RSVP: Respond via e-mail within 24 hours. Include your phone number, and you will receive a call from the director with all the details.

PS: If you tell, your costars' roles will be cut.

"There's something else," she says, pulling out a 4 x 6 photograph. It's a picture of five dolls. They're all lined up against a crude cement wall: a guy doll dressed in dark clothes, with lots of silver jewelry; a girl doll with weird patchy hair and shrouded in dark layers; two more guy dolls (one holds a guitar; the other one reminds me of a surfer dude with his scruffy blond hair); and a pretty dark-skinned girl with a smiling face.

"These represent the missing contestants, don't they?" I say, more as a statement than a question.

"And if we want to save them, we have to go to this." She nods to the invite. "We have to follow his rules or else their roles will get cut."

"Meaning?" I ask, fearing I know the answer.

Ivy pulls out her phone and opens it up to the Nightmare Elf's last e-mail. She hits REPLY.

"Holy Hell!!" I pull her fingers away from the screen. "Haven't you ever heard of impulse control? Let's talk about this."

"What is there to talk about? Are you with me on this or not?" She raises her eyebrow, à la Tippi Hedren in Alfred Hitchcock's *The Birds*.

"By 'with me,' do you mean not calling the police?"

"By 'with me,' I mean saving the others once and for all." Ivy glares at me like a possessed vampire junkie on blood-flavored crack.

"Look—" I take a deep breath. "It's three o'clock in the morning. We're standing in the middle of a rainstorm, in the middle of a parking lot. And I'm not even wearing public-viewing-worthy PJs." I flash her the hole in one of my kisses, right over my left butt cheek.

"So..."

"So, let's go back inside, change our clothes, get some shut-eye. We can rethink things in the morning when we're not so saturated."

"Except that every moment we wait, the clock just keeps on ticking."

I wouldn't be surprised if she can hear the ticking inside her head, like a time bomb about to go off. "We have twenty-four hours to respond," I remind her. "So, what do you say we use at least six or seven of them? I can't be responsible for any decisions made before ten on a Saturday morning with a stomach devoid of home fries and sausage links."

My comment takes her off guard, and the tension in her face releases. Game point: I've won this round.

IVY

I WAIT UNTIL TAYLOR NODS OFF BEFORE HEADING out to the hallway. Sitting on the floor with my back pressed against the wall, I stare at the photo of the dolls, desperate for some clue. The background is dark. The dolls look vintage with their wide, haunted eyes and their dirty, scratched-up faces.

I check my phone, knowing I have at least a couple of missed messages—two missed calls from Apple and a text from Core telling me to check in. I text both that all is well at the food fest.

The e-mail from the Nightmare Elf is up on the screen. I hit REPLY, thinking about all the other questions I might ask him:

Why my parents? Is it true that my dad went superquick, like the medical examiner said? What were my mom's final words? And are Parker and the others still alive?

I run the T-shirt bracelet over my cheek, imagining that Parker can feel it somehow. The reply box still open, I type in my cell phone number. My finger trembles over the SEND tab. Should I? Shouldn't I?

Finally, I press SEND, feeling a wave of relief. Only now can I get some rest.

There's a vibrating sensation inside my palm; it jolts me awake. I open my eyes and sit up. I'm back in Taylor's room, on the futon. Taylor's still asleep in her bed.

The phone clenched in my hand, the vibrating continues. The screen says PRIVATE CALLER. I click it on, moving out into the hallway. The brightness of the overhead lights shocks my eyes.

"Hello, Princess." His deep-throated voice sends shivers all over my skin. "It's been a long time, hasn't it?"

My head whirs. There's a swirl of darkness behind my eyes, making everything feel hazy and thick. "What do you want?"

"Oh, but this isn't about what *I* want. This is about what *you* want, isn't it, Princess? You gave me your number. You looked Taylor up. *You* reached out to *me*. I'm assuming that by going to such great lengths, you must really want to reclaim your role."

"My role," I repeat, at a sudden loss for words.

"You want to be my star again, don't you, Princess?"

I reach for the keys inside my pocket and run my finger over the sharpest one—not as pointed as a knife, but it has a tip, and manages to soothe. *I'm in control. I still have choices.* "Where are the others?"

"It's enchanting to hear your voice."

"*Where are the others?*" I insist.

"By others, do you mean your costars?"

"Okay," I say. There's a hitch in my throat.

"You'll have to see, my honeybee."

A door creaks open at the end of the hallway. Three girls emerge wearing matching heart-patterned pajamas. They're giggling as they move toward the stairwell, seemingly without a care in the world.

I look at the time; it's 7:32 a.m. "How do you know that I won't go to the police?"

He laughs—a cackling sound that reverberates inside my bones. "Because I know you, April. I've been watching you for a long, long time, internalizing your every choice. You were desperate enough a year ago to enter my contest, despite how scared you were by it, just to put old ghosts to rest. You're even more desperate now."

My breath stops. My skin ices over.

"Cat got your tongue?" There's amusement in his voice. "Do you miss your fine prince, my princess? Would you like to see him again? I have an inkling he might like that too."

"Is Parker still alive?"

"Not so quick, my sugar stick. I believe you'd asked me a question. Do you remember what it was?"

"Why did you wait so long?"

"Because you're like that fine bottle of wine just waiting to be uncorked. It would've been a waste to indulge too soon. One needs to be patient until things have properly aged and ripened. Alas, from the very first time I saw you, I knew you'd be the perfect star. I hope you'll be my star again."

"Will it mean getting to see the others?"

"So long as you keep things between us. Do I make myself clear?"

"How do I know they're still alive?"

"You don't. That's a leap of faith you'll have to take."

"And if I don't take that leap?"

"Then you'll never know if you could've done something, saved someone, silenced the screaming inside your head."

There's a jumping sensation in my gut, a rushing sensation through my veins. "What do I need to do? Where do I need to go?"

"Ivy?" Taylor asks. She's standing right behind me. The door to her room is open. There's a confused expression on her face.

I hold up my finger, asking for a second.

"Who are you talking to?" she persists.

"Just give me a minute," I insist, cupping over the mouthpiece.

"Holy shit. It's him, isn't it? You totally e-mailed him, didn't you? Even though we agreed to wait."

The phone clicks. He hung up.

Ticktock, ticktock.

Boom.

TAYLOR

IVY IS TOTALLY GOING TO BLOW. STILL, SHE ACCEPTS my invitation for fresh air. We go outside and walk across the footbridge, finally ending up at the rec hall—a favorite spot on campus. There are cushy chairs, snack machines, game tables, and an espresso bar with ten degrees of boldness (for those particularly rough cramming sessions).

Ivy and I gravitate to the espresso bar. She brews herself a #10, while I go for a #3 with extra cream and two packets of sugar, and we sit on a couch, overlooking the foosball tables.

"Look," I begin, unable to take her silent treatment for one more sip, "I get that you're upset, but I thought the deal was that we weren't going to do anything until morning."

"The killer was about to tell me what I needed to do."

"What you needed to do *to what?*"

"I'm sure he'll call me back. He has my number. He knows how to reach me." Her cell phone's clenched in her hand.

"We need to go to the police," I tell her for the umpteenth time.

"No," she barks. "You need to promise me that you won't."

"I can't." I sigh. "I've already surpassed my limit on screwups regarding this case."

"Give me at least a week."

"A week to do what?"

"Research." She pinches the skin on her kneecap. "I just want a chance to go through the clues on my own before turning them over to anyone."

"You do realize that pawing over physical clues is, like, number one on the how-to-sabotage-the-evidence list, don't you?"

"I know what I'm doing."

"Oh, right, because you binge-watch *CSI?*"

"The killer knows what he's doing too," she continues, ignoring my jab. "He's way too smart to leave fingerprints or DNA."

"Are you really willing to take that risk?"

"I think you owe me a week."

"Why? Because everything's all my fault? Because you obviously blame me too?"

"Because I'm asking *you*—someone who was able to dodge the worst weekend of my life, and arguably the worst weekend of the five other missing contest winners—to wait."

Her words are sharp. They form a knife that stabs into my back. "Three days," I say to compromise. "After that, I'm going to the police. And I'm going to tell them everything."

"Three days," she repeats, extending her hand to shake on it.

I give her a hug instead. Her arms wrap around my shoulders, but the embrace falls short of the one from last night when she first arrived—that palpable sort of connection.

"It'll all be fine," she mutters.

I know she's totally trying to bullshit me—that things are about as fine as fuzzy bacon bits—but I take her lie anyway.

From the Journal of E.W.

Grade 7, August Preparatory School

WINTER 1972

I can see a face inside my head: a blond-haired boy with freckles and a pointed nose. I roll over in bed. My shades are drawn. My heart is racing. There's still three more hours until people start waking up.

I reach for my inhaler, flashing back to cold sweats and panic attacks, sitting alone in my bedroom at home, with the door locked and the light out, able to hear noises out in the hallway—footsteps, door knocks, floors creaking, bells jangling.

My mind told me that it was Mother making the noises. I could hear her evil little-girl giggle, after all. But every other part of me was convinced that it was the ghost of Johnny, outside my bedroom, coming to get me.

I click on my night table light. Everything appears normal—dresser, desk, chair, bookcase, journal—but it still feels like someone's here. I lean over the side of the bed to check beneath it. Empty.

It's been like this all week. Whenever I close my eyes at night, I can see that boy's face. I asked the man in charge of the rooms if I could switch mine, but he said no changes—that if he changed one, then everybody would be asking. I wonder if my grandparents are paying him extra for that.

Last night, when I got up to check the door, I could've sworn the temperature in the room had dropped by at least twenty degrees. I tried the knob. A good sign: it was still locked. An even better sign: I was able to unlock it, unlike years before in my bedroom back home.

I closed the door, turned toward the bed again, and felt my heart come to a sudden stop. There was something sticking up from behind my pillow—some kind of paper. I moved closer to see what it was, thinking that maybe a page had fallen out from my journal or that I'd misplaced a handout from one of my classes.

I moved to stand just a couple of feet from the headboard, and the answer became clear. It was a page from an August Prep yearbook. I scanned the photos, somehow knowing what I would find. And I was right. There was a photo of the blond-haired boy with the freckles and pointed nose—the same boy that's been popping up inside my mind.

Ricky Slater.

Ivy

IT'S FORTY-EIGHT HOURS LATER, AND I STILL HAVEN'T heard back from the killer. And so I've been searching online, trying to find images of the dolls from the photo. Does he own them? Where are they from? What year were they made? What are the chances that I can find them together as a collection?

Dr. Tully called about an hour ago, reminding me about our outpatient therapy deal, which I took as a definite threat. And so that's exactly where I am—in the hospital parking lot, having just exited my car. I step through the doors of the mental health wing just as my phone vibrates in my pocket.

I check the screen: PRIVATE CALLER. My heart instantly clenches.

"Are you coming?" a girl asks, holding the elevator open for me.

I shake my head and click on the phone. "Hello?" I cover my ear and move toward the exit door, looking back out over the parking lot. "*Hello?*"

"Good evening, Princess." His voice sends a shockwave through my body.

"What do you want?" I ask him.

"This isn't about what *I* want, remember? Are you alone?"

I look back over my shoulder, just as someone emerges from the stairwell and then moves past me through the exit doors. "Sort of."

"Sort of isn't good enough, Princess. Go someplace private."

"Okay," I mutter, heading outside. I cross the road in front of the entrance, and then hurry across the parking lot, fumbling to retrieve my keys from inside my pocket. I go to get back inside my car, but the doors are locked. I jam the wrong key into the lock before finding the right one.

Back inside my car, I lock the door behind me. "I'm alone now," I tell him, all out of breath. The overhead streetlamps shine through my windshield, making me feel exposed. My head aches. I haven't taken my meds.

"Good, because our conversations should only be between

the two of us. Do you understand that, April? One word to any-one else—any lofty plans to conspire with the police—and your costars will be cut. Do I make myself clear?"

"Very. I get it. It's just you and me. What do I need to do? Where do I need to go?"

"I've actually come to you. Do you have paper and a pen?"

I reach into my bag and pull out one of my many notebooks. "Okay."

"I trust that you'll keep these notes between us as well. One wrong move . . ."

"If you wanted to keep things so private, why did you contact me while I was at Taylor's?"

"You're a very smart girl, you know that?" His voice is soft and slow.

"She wants to go to the police."

"But I'm sure you've convinced her otherwise. I know you, April. I can predict your every move. And if you ever let me down, I'll find out and simply adjust accordingly. I always have a plan in place—an insurance policy that safeguards myself against disloyalty."

"You don't deserve loyalty."

"I may not deserve it, but still you're extending it to me, aren't you? By keeping our little secret. You must really want to see your costars."

"Where do I need to go?"

"Drive northeast on Route 87 from Sturbridge, Maine. Get off at exit 4 and take a right on Chelsea Avenue. Park in the lot behind Chalmers Chocolate Factory."

I write everything down, almost unable to imagine going through with any of these plans.

"When you get to Chalmers," he continues, "cross the street to the bus stop and take the number 452 going south. Get out at the Lancaster Road stop. You'll see a field; cross it."

My pulse races as I scribble down his every word. This is just too surreal. It can't possibly be happening.

"When you come to the other side of the field, there will be a small boat attached to a dock," he says. "Use it to cross the lake. Look for a tall maple tree with a yellow scarf tied to the branches. There you will find further instructions. Goodbye for now, my princess."

"Wait," I stammer. "When am I supposed to go there? When do I need to do this?"

"*The sooner the better to see a fine letter.*"

"A fine letter?"

"Don't wait too long. *Ticktock. Ticktock.*"

The ticking's inside me as well, clouding over my mind, making everything feel urgent, broken, dire, desperate.

"This offer is only available for a limited time," he chides.

"How limited?"

"By the count of one, my honeybun." The phone clicks. He's hung up.

Ivy

I SPEND THE NEXT COUPLE OF HOURS DRIVING around, trying to sort out my manic thoughts. I pull over a couple of times—to respond to a text from Apple and then to answer a call from Core: "Therapy went fine," I tell him.

"Are you on your way home?"

"I'm spending the night at Candy's, from the Depot. She broke up with her boyfriend and now she's a wreck. She asked if I'd stay the night." Even though I no longer live at home, I know that he and Apple check up on me. They notice when my car isn't parked in the driveway.

"Aunt Tillie should be back from her trip on Monday," he says. "But you know that if you ever get lonely, you can always come home."

"I know. And thanks. I'll call you in the morning."

We hang up and I recheck my screen. Miko sent me a text: "You looked out of it this AM. The flu? I made chicken soup. LMK if I can drop it off."

Everyone's looking out for me. I have such a cheering squad on my side. And yet I feel so desperately alone.

I rest my head against the steering wheel, resisting the urge to bang it. What did the killer mean when he said "by the count of one"? One day? One week? It couldn't possibly have been one hour. He would've said if there was that much of a ticking clock . . . *right?*

In the same vein, I doubt he'd give me one week. Too much could happen in such a lapse in time—I could devise too much of a plan, become distracted, get others involved, or even change my mind.

It's one day. I'm sure of it. Just enough time for me to pack up some stuff and come up with an excuse for being away.

I drive onto the Gringle College campus and park in the lot by Taylor's dorm, wondering if coming here wasn't a big mistake.

It's raining again. The droplets pound against the glass, making it hard to see. I pull out my phone and call Taylor's number.

"Hey," she answers.

"I hope I didn't wake you."

"Are you kidding? I never go to bed before eleven; there's way too much goodness on TV, and speaking of . . . have you seen this week's episode of *Relationship 9-1-1*?"

"I doubt it."

"Wait, are you okay?"

"I'm fine, why?"

"I don't know. I guess you sound a little lost."

I look at my reflection in the window glass—tired eyes, pasty face, hair pulled back in a messy braid. "You'll never guess where I am right now."

"Paris? Sitting beside a hot French guy at some chic café? In which case, why are you calling me?"

"I'm right outside your building."

"Seriously?"

My breath fogs up the window. In the condensation, I write Parker's name.

"Um, *hello*. Earth to Ivy."

"I'm here. I mean, I'm *really* here. I can see the entrance doors to your dormitory," through the letters in Parker's name.

"Well, then what are you waiting for? Get your spontaneous ass up here."

"Okay," I say, relieved by her cheery disposition. Just hearing it, despite the darkness—in the car, in my heart—my spirits lift.

TAYLOR

I OPEN THE DOOR OF MY ROOM. IVY'S STANDING
there. Her clothes are wet. The mascara has run down her cheeks.

"Get in here," I tell her. "Let me find you some dry clothes." I
fish an acorn-pattered bodysuit from my basket of clean clothes.
"Feeling squirrelly?"

"Why do you have that?"

"Because sometimes I feel like a nut."

She can't help but smile, despite how deflated she seems. Meanwhile, I continue to dig, finally finding a ho-hum pair of sweats.
"These good?"

"I'm actually fine," she says, twitching from the cold.

"You look about as fine as the monster zit on my forehead." I force the sweats into her arms and point her to the bathroom down the hall.

She comes back only a few minutes later, all changed, and sits down on the edge of the futon. "He called me again."

"He, as in our resident psychotic killer."

She nods. "He gave me directions—for what I need to do, for where I need to go—to find the others."

"And where *are* the directions?" I ask her.

"I'm keeping them someplace safe."

Translation: *I don't trust you enough to say.* "There's no place safer than with the authorities," I tell her.

"He wants you to join me too—the killer, I mean—to find the others, to star in his film."

"Did he actually say that?"

"It was more of what he *didn't* say."

"Call me crazy, but there's something about the words *killer* and *join* in that gives me the heebie-jeebies."

"This could be your opportunity," she says, "to right the past, to show everyone you're not selfish the way they think."

"The only opportunity is the one that involves calling the police. It's nutty that we haven't already." I mean, yeah, it sucks that I've become a social leper, but I'm hardly willing to risk my life to change that.

"You promised me three days."

"And so I'm obviously a total idiot."

"You made that promise because deep down you know I'm right. All the horror movies say so. The police are never the ones who find the killer in the end. They simply show up after the climax—after all the hard work has already been done."

The girl *does* have a point. But still, "I'm going to the police first thing tomorrow morning."

She stands up from the futon. Her forehead looks sweaty. "I'm sorry. It was stupid of me to come here. I just thought..." She lets out a sigh. "I actually don't know what I was thinking. To anyone else, this must seem crazy."

"Ivy—don't go." I stand up too. "I mean, truly don't go. Let's just drive down to the police and tell them everything we know."

"I can't." There are tears in her eyes. "I have to see this through—for my parents, for Parker and the others, and for myself. He'll continue to haunt me otherwise. I'll always be waiting for him to strike if I don't." She starts to go for the door. "I'm really sorry that I bothered you."

"Wait, are you kidding?" I move to block her from the door. "You're not going anywhere. You're spending the night here—on my pickled futon. Harry wouldn't have it any other way." I grab Handyman Harry from a heap of random stuff on my desk. "He hasn't stopped talking about you since your last visit." I wink. "He's been dying to get you into bed."

Finally, Ivy smiles. I've cracked the code, broken through her wall. I grab an extra pillow and some blankets from the closet, and start making up the futon before she can try to weasel her way out.

Surprisingly, she follows my lead and settles into bed. I'm just about to slip on my eye mask when I notice that she's rolled onto her side, facing the wall, and that her shoulders are slightly jittering.

"Ivy?" I gaze over at Handyman Harry, knowing that we're so far beyond what even he is able to repair. And so I do the only thing I can. I get up and move to snuggle in beside her. I stroke her back, the same way that Darcy Conner did for me, four years ago, after the Starbound Dance Competition, when my ex-boyfriend Max dumped me for Paula Perfect Pirouette with the huge beaver teeth. "Do you want to talk some more?" When she doesn't answer, I pull a tear-soaked strand of hair from in front of her eyes. "We can just sleep on things for now." I wait until she falls asleep; only then do I go back to bed.

IVY

SOMETIME AFTER SIX IN THE MORNING, WITH TAYLOR
still asleep, I get up and write her a note:

Dear Taylor,

I haven't had a lot of friends in my lifetime, but spending time with you, I can see how much I've missed. I'll call you just as soon as I can. Thanks so much for everything.

Love,

Ivy

I set the note on her night table, and then open the door to leave, accidentally catching my bag strap on the knob. The fabric makes a ripping sound.

I turn to look.

Luckily, she remains sleeping, her eye mask still in place.

I move down the hallway. The dorm is quiet at this hour. A cleaning woman in the lobby asks if I'm going for an early run, but I'm too uptight to answer.

It's still somewhat dark out. The sun is tucked behind a cluster of clouds, making the day feel even more ominous. I hurry to my car, get inside, and turn up the heat. Sitting with my head pressed against the steering wheel, I try to concentrate on just my breath, but it's balled up inside my chest, pushing against my ribs.

I check my cell phone. There's only twenty-five percent of the charge left. My fingers tremble as I reach inside the glove box and pull out my wool scarf. I unravel what's tucked inside it.

A knife. The blade is six inches long. The handle has a nice grip—slip-proof, hard plastic. I turn it over in my hand, reminded of its ample weight, assured by its curved tip.

Ticktock, ticktock.

I grab my phone and text Core that Candy's still in a bad way, and so I'll be spending the day trying to cheer her up. The mere idea that I could cheer up anyone should be a dead giveaway.

I text Candy next, knowing she has the day off: "Cover for

me if Apple calls. I'm at your place today, and btw I stayed there last night too. I'll explain later. Big thanks. XOXO." I power my phone down to conserve the battery, pull out my notebook, and flip open to the page with the instructions.

Route 87 is a two-lane highway that goes on forever. There aren't many people out this way. Maybe it's because it's still early. More likely it's because there isn't anything out here. He's sending me someplace desolate.

The early morning frost covers the road, making the pavement glisten. I peek in the rearview mirror a couple of times, feeling like I'm being followed, but the only cars on the road with me are so far back. Am I driving too fast? I look around for a speed limit sign. Sixty-five. My speedometer says eighty. I need to slow down.

More than two hours later and I finally reach exit 4. I take it and go right on Chelsea Avenue, spotting the chocolate factory immediately—a wide abandoned brick building with a crooked sign over the front entrance that reads CHALMERS CHOCOLATE, in what once must've been pretty red cursive. There's tagging along the side, and most of the windows have been boarded up.

I pull into the back lot and park, as instructed, behind the building. Aside from a tiny food market, a gas station/hotdog stand, and a drugstore that advertises check-cashing and lottery tickets, the area looks vacant.

The bus stop is across the street, just like he said. I peer down the road, able to see a bus in the distance, getting closer. I squint hard, trying to see what bus it is. As if by fate—my coming here, my doing this—the number 452 comes into view.

I stuff the knife inside my bag, grab my cell phone, and hurry across the street, knowing that I'm much more vulnerable on foot.

The bus doors open with a thwack and I step inside. There are only two other riders, neither of whom makes eye contact. I tell the driver that I'll be getting off at the Lancaster stop, hoping that he remembers my face.

I take a seat toward the front, reminding myself that it isn't too late. I can still call the police. Maybe they can hatch a plan; some undercover person who looks like me could go through the motions of getting to this very place. But then what if the clues end up being dead ends, once again? Would I get another chance?

I close my eyes, able to hear Detective Thomas's words darting across my brain, constricting the air in my lungs: *"You're, what . . . three weeks out of a mental hospital? How many times have you called and/or come to see me since then? Fourteen times in five weeks."*

Nearly ninety minutes later, after passing through miles of farm and conservation land, we reach Lancaster Road. I gaze out the window. There's nothing here.

"Are you sure this is where you want to go?" the driver asks.

"I'm sure," I say, able to feel the words in my chest—a sharp, jabbing pain.

I exit the bus. The doors fold shut. The air is cold. My breath is visible. The bus drives away, leaving me completely alone. I pull my phone out of my bag and power it back on. I have a bunch of missed calls from Taylor, not to mention twenty-two percent of my charge left—still plenty of juice to make a call. I look all around, feeling as if I'm being watched. The road is narrow. Woods border it on one side. On the other side is a grass field, just like the killer said.

Keeping the phone gripped in my hand, I begin across the field, headed for a rock wall, wondering what this area used to be. There's a dilapidated farmhouse that borders the field; its windows have all been boarded up. An old, rusted tractor, missing all of its tires, is parked in the driveway. There's also a windmill in the distance and an old barn.

Finally I get to the rock wall, but there's another field on the other side of it. I recheck the instructions; there's no mention of two fields, but still I begin across it. After about twenty more minutes of walking, I'm finally able to see it.

A lake.

A dock.

A small boat.

I check my phone again. I have twenty percent of charge left, but no bars. There's no reception. Should I turn back around? My brain tells me yes, but I move to the boat anyway and sit down inside it.

Using the tip of my knife, I scratch my initials into the wood as evidence that I was here. I should've done the same at the bus stop, should've left something behind on the bus . . . a bracelet, a lip balm.

The wooded land that surrounds the lake is thick and vast. I undock the boat, grab the oar, and start to paddle out, searching for a tree with a yellow scarf, keeping my focus on a grouping of trees directly across from the dock.

At last, I spot it. A long yellow scarf tied to a low branch. It flaps in the breeze, as if waving me over.

My shoulder aches as I paddle through the water at full speed. The front of the boat smacks into the land, propelling me forward.

I get out, tie the boat to a stump, and move toward the tree, searching for a clue.

The scarf continues to waver. There doesn't appear to be anything tied to it or written on the underside. I untie it from the branch, suspecting there might be a note hidden beneath the knot.

But there isn't. The scarf is clean.

I look down, between my feet. The ground's uneven. The dirt's been overturned. There must be something buried.

I crouch down and begin to dig, using a pointed rock. The dirt comes up easily. The muscles in my forearms throb from working furiously.

At last I find something.

The rock makes a clank sound.

There's a hard metal surface.

I continue to dig, lifting a box out of the ground. It's about the size of a carton of eggs, about the weight of one too. I jiggle it back and forth, able to hear the slight shifting of something inside.

My pulse races as I go to open the box, fumbling with the latch. I lift the lid; the hinges squeak.

There's an envelope inside. My name is scribbled across the front. I pick it up, noticing more envelopes beneath it—a whole stack of them—all with my name, all sealed, and all with the same handwriting across the fronts: block letters, slightly slanted.

I tear the top one open and pull out a sheet of paper. At first I assume that it's going to be further instructions.

But it's not.

It's a letter.

To me.

Dear Ivy,

I'm not really sure where to begin, except maybe with the obvious. There hasn't been a day that's gone by that I haven't thought about you at least a dozen times.

I worry that you didn't make it to safety. I wonder where you are and what you're doing, and what you imagine about the others and me. I also think about the status of things. Are the police close? Did they find enough clues? Did your nightmares ever stop? Or are they even worse now?

I replay the same scene inside my head: the one where the police bust in and find the others and me. You're there too, cutting my ropes, helping me up, leading me outside. I picture a bright blue sky, puffy clouds, fallen autumn leaves, and ambulance trucks in the distance with medics running toward us.

And I picture you: your lips pressed together with concern; your eyes tearing up with relief; your hands wrapped around mine, almost unwilling to let me go. Again.

I wish that I could see you, and hold you, just like I did in your room that first night. I miss you, Ivy. A lot. And so I'm writing you this letter, and I'll write you a bunch more—as many as I have to—to remind myself of hope. It's easy to forget it exists—at least it is for me right now.

Love,
Parker

I reread the letter, my heart pounding, my body quaking. This seriously can't be real. It must be part of a setup.

"Ivy?" a voice calls from behind me.

I turn to look, startled to find Taylor.

Still wearing her sweats from last night, she has a confused expression on her face. "What are you . . . ?" Her voice trails off. "You just left. Again." She stops from speaking to study my face.

I open my mouth, wanting to answer, desperate to ask my own questions too: What is she doing here? How did she find me? Did she get instructions from the killer as well? But instead of saying anything, I remain silent, the words stuck in my throat.

Taylor's eyes move to the metal box, and then to the hole I dug, and finally to the letter in my hand. And that's when something in her brain clicks. Her eyes soften. The muscles in her mouth loosen.

She gets it—maybe not the "*it*." But she gets that something big has happened. And that's obviously "it" enough.

She comes and wraps her arms around me without another word. Meanwhile, I'm crying so hard now—and not just because of the letter, but also because of her kindness—that I have virtually no words left.

From the Journal of E.W.

Grade 7, August Preparatory School

WINTER 1972

I shouldn't be awake. It's the middle of the night, but something startled me and I sat up in bed and looked all around.

There are numbers on the wall, in front of my bed. Big, small, tall, fat. Numbers. Scribbled. Glowing in the dark. Making my muscles twitch.

I click on my night table lamp. The numbers disappear right away. Relief. I can breathe.

Should I turn the light back off? No. I don't want to know if the numbers are still there.

I've been waking up every night. Each time it's something new: whispering, laughing, knocking, the creaking sound of hinges. Sometimes I'm not fully awake and think that it's Mother trying to scare me. But then I remind myself that she's locked up for good, punished for setting the house on fire with me inside, trying to blame it all on the ghost of Johnny.

Sometimes I wish that I'd burned to death that day. Other times I feel like I am on fire—like every inch of me is singeing, and that no amount of water will make me feel normal. Whatever normal feels like.

I don't want to go to sleep anymore. I lie awake in bed, feeling like a little kid again, back home, shaking beneath the bedcovers, reaching for my inhaler, hating and wanting Mother both at once.

I told the man in charge of the rooms about all the weird stuff that's been happening, but he said it was probably just my imagination, that a lot of the kids complain about the same kinds of stuff.

I asked Tray across the hall if weird stuff happened to him too. He said that one time he heard knocking on all the walls of his room, and that he now sleeps with the light on. I will too. I also have a statue of Mother Mary, a prayer candle, and some rosary beads. I stole it all from the chapel when Father Pranas wasn't looking. I hold Mary tight as I close my eyes for bed, praying that Ricky won't come, but he always does, just like Mother. She always came too, bringing stories of Johnny along with her.

IVY'S FACE IS FLUSHED. HER BODY'S SHAKING.
There's a tear-soaked letter clenched in her hand. I pry it free,
more than curious to know what prompted such a reaction.

The letter's from Parker—*major* reactor. "Do you think it's
real?" I ask, ever the pessimist.

"How did you find me?" she asks, in lieu of an answer.

"Easy. You woke me up. I followed you here."

"*What?*" She looks confused, like I'm speaking in special code.

"Okay, so maybe it wasn't *that* easy, now that I think about it.
By the time I got out to the parking lot, you were already pulling

away. Normally I'd have just turned around and gone back inside, but let's face it: you were acting like an escaped mental patient last night—and not in a cute come-eat-Checkers-with-me sort of way; more like in an I've-got-a-fresh-pack-of-razor-blades-at-the-ready kind of way. Bottom line: I couldn't *not* follow you. You're just lucky that I happened to have a full tank of gas."

"You followed the bus too?"

"I followed the bus, I followed your car."

"But you didn't try to stop me?"

"Believe me, it wasn't for lack of trying. First of all, I called you, like, a bagillion times, but it kept going straight to voicemail. And then you were driving so fast that I nearly lost you twice. And PS, you ignored my honking. By the time I pulled into Chalmers, you were already boarding the bus, and I was sixty minutes over trying to snag your attention. My curiosity was way too piqued at that point to interrupt you on your mysterious mission. I was determined to see just *where* you were headed and why. I totally thought I was bagged once you got off the bus, but I was able to pull in behind an old boarded-up barn. It was kind of exciting, actually. I felt like Veronica Mars."

"Did you cross the fields?"

"Well, um, yeah." I feel my eyes grow big. "I'm *here*, aren't I? Of course, I didn't go on foot. While you opted to walk, I drove—at least as far as I could, that is. I ended up taking a road that wrapped around the side of the field, keeping my eye on you the whole time, Ms. I'm So Hyper-focused That I Don't Even Notice When People Are Following Me. Not exactly the best quality for someone who claims to have killers after her, FYI. Anyhoo"—I pause for a breath—"I parked my car somewhere around that rock wall. I was almost tempted to try phoning you then, but I left my cell in my car and didn't want to risk losing you by going back to get it."

"He's still alive," she says, nodding to her box of buried treasure.

"Right, because dead boys don't write letters. The whole transparency thing makes it nearly impossible. It gives new meaning to the expression 'can't get a grip.'"

"I'm *serious*," she scolds me. "It sounds like the others are alive too—or at least some of them."

"How do you know that these letters are really from Parker? That this isn't someone's warped idea of fun?"

"Just look," she says, handing me another letter.

Dear Ivy,

The person who's taken me found a bunch of the letters I wrote to you. He ripped up a couple, kept a few, and then encouraged me to write you more—with a number of stipulations, that is.

At first I felt a spark of hope, picturing you someplace safe—like inside your bedroom, snuggled beneath the covers—reading them. But when I stopped to really think about it, that hope morphed into something else—fear, anger—because I figured he'd be using the letters against me somehow. Or, worse, against you.

I'm supposed to tell you that if you want to see me or any of the others again, you have to come here and find us. I wish that weren't the plan. I wish I never had to write that sentence. I hope you'll never have to see it.

Be safe, Be smart, Love,
Parker

I look up from the letter. "The boy has a way with words, doesn't he? But can he also make a decent breakfast?"

"He's being told what to write," she says, ignoring my attempt at humor.

"Not everything. Plus, it sounds as if he started writing to you on his own—like it was his idea to begin with."

"I've been writing to him too." Her face turns pink, seemingly in love with the idea that they're both on the same letter-writing wavelength (despite the fact that people are missing—ahem, *assumed dead*—and that we're standing in the middle of nowhere).

She spends the next several minutes poring over more letters—until I can't take it any longer and have to ask the obvious. "So, what *is* all of this? What does it mean?"

"It means, this is it. The real deal. I'm going to find the others."

"Like, *now*?" I ask, the light finally dawning—the remote location, Ivy's sense of urgency, the freaky phone call she talked about last night.

"Now," she says, her eyes completely focused, blink-less, as if there isn't a doubt in her mind.

"*Ivy?*" I shout. "I mean, holy freaking freaksterville. This is crazy."

"No." She shakes her head. "Crazy is not taking this opportunity. Crazy is blowing it by telling too many people. Crazy is knowing that a killer is after me and doing nothing about it."

"Crazy is *this*," I snap.

She goes to open another letter, but I stop her before she can, snatching the entire stack, and thus revealing the hidden jewel. A handheld tape player sits at the bottom of the box. "Jackpot!" I declare, picking it up. I push EJECT to pop out the audiocassette. Scribbled across the front are the words PLAY ME.

Ivy takes the tape and studies the label, looking at it from different angles, as if it's an alien object dropped down from outer space. After a few moments, she puts it back in and pushes PLAY. The tape is staticky at first, adding to the whole creepy vibe.

"Hello, Princess," a voice seeps out, cutting through the static and making the surreal *real*. "I hope this finds you well. If you've come this far, I'll assume you'll travel a little farther. Do you see the path that cuts through the woods, not far from where you're sitting?"

"Right there." Ivy points.

"Take it," he says.

"Wait, how does he know that we're sitting?" She looks all around.

"It's a tape," I remind her. "He's assuming that you're sitting. I wouldn't overanalyze it."

"When you come to a swamp area," the male voice continues, "the path will fork. Go to the right."

I grab the recorder and push PAUSE. "We seriously need to think things through, because let's just say, for argument's sake, that you continue to indulge this psychopath by playing his twisted game. Then what?"

Ivy responds by taking the recorder back. She gets up and begins down the path, leaving me in the proverbial dust.

"Um, *hello?*" I call out. "You're not bailing on me, are you? Particularly after I followed you here and hiked around a lake, sans boat, sacrificing my brand-new pair of Uggs."

Ivy turns to face me again, gazing down at my sacrificial boots. "What do you mean?"

"I mean, I'm coming with you," I say, before I can think twice about it.

"Excuse me?" she asks, as if I'm speaking in secret code again.

I stare out into the woods, flashing back to that day at the Dark House, scurrying past Natalie's room, and then climbing out a window and fleeing into the woods without ever looking back.

"Taylor?"

"Who else is going to tip you off to all the standard cliché horror gimmicks? I'll be able to smell the evil clowns and menacing elves from a mile away."

Ivy studies my face in anticipation, as if a giant anaconda might come bursting out of my mouth. "Are you sure?"

I nod, unsure, and she comes and wraps her arms around me. Her body quivers like the leaves on the trees all around us. And suddenly it seems so obvious—why the killer chose her in the first place.

"You're, like, the quintessential scream queen," I tell her, taking a step back. "The girl who fights for the good of others, despite the consequences; whose bravery trumps her fears."

"Bravery or stupidity?"

"I'm not like that," I tell her. "That's the difference between you and me."

"Except you *are* like that," she argues. "I mean, you're here, aren't you?"

I shake my head, fairly confident that while she's the heroine, I'm the character who thinks she's smarter than everyone else but actually gets slaughtered en route to escape.

Somehow despite knowing that, I follow her down the path.

Ivy

TAYLOR AND I TAKE THE PATH THAT CUTS THROUGH
the woods, walking for what feels like miles. I know she doesn't
want to be here. And part of me wants to tell her to go, but I hold
that part in, grateful to have her with me.

"Hey, aren't we looking for that?" She points to a swamp.

I nod and push PLAY.

"Once you find the swamp," the voice says, "it'll just be a little
bit farther."

I push PAUSE again, my mind reeling with questions. How long will it take for someone to find my car behind the chocolate factory? At what point will my family contact Candy and figure out that I lied? How long after that will the police go into my e-mail to put all the pieces together?

"Ivy?" Taylor's several steps in front of me now. "We're going the right way, aren't we?"

I wonder where she's parked—if it's in a spot that has cell reception, if someone will be able to trace her phone's whereabouts.

"Are you still with me?" she asks.

I nod and push PLAY again.

"I'm really excited to see you, Princess." His voice is soft and deep; the words come out slowly. "Very soon now. Just keep on walking."

The path narrows. There are tall, vine-like bushes on both sides of us. The tops of them form a ceiling above our heads, and we have to keep ducked.

"What's he saying now?" Taylor asks.

The path winds left and right, forming a maze. Branches stick out in my path, pulling at my hair, scraping against my cheeks. I try to keep up, but Taylor quickens her pace, hell-bent on getting to the end.

"Just a little bit farther," the voice reminds us, as if talking in real time.

Several yards in front of me, Taylor lifts a branch and peeks outward. "Holy shitster!" she declares, cupping her hand over her mouth.

"What is it?" My heart sinks.

She waves me over, still keeping her eyes locked on whatever's out there, beyond these shrubs.

I move slowly, my heart pounding.

"Are you there yet, Princess?" The soft purr of his voice sends shivers all over my skin.

I join Taylor, by her side, and gaze upward. A huge, Gothic-looking building sits in the distance behind an iron gate. With multiple pointed roofs and a cobblestone courtyard in the center, overgrown ivy crawls up the sides of the building, twists around the front pillars, and clogs up a chimney. "What is this place?" The windows have been boarded up, but both the gate and entrance doors are wide open. "Someone wants us to go inside."

"Of course they do," Taylor says. "Come right in, step right up, and you too can drop off the face of the earth, just like your fellow contestants."

"You don't have to come with me," I tell her. "I'll understand if you don't."

Taylor nods, perhaps considering her options.

I try to stay focused, wondering what this building once was. A rich person's home? A castle? There isn't any graffiti or tagging, so either no one knows the building's here, or nobody comes out this far.

"It must be ancient," she says, pointing toward the entrance. There are gargoyles over the door, looking down at the front steps. There's also a garden gazebo and what appears to be a chapel attached to one side of the building. "Maybe it was once a convent or monastery," she guesses.

The building itself sits in the middle of a sprawling field, with woods just behind it. There's a dirt path that branches out from what was probably once a driveway, but there are no roads that lead here.

"Welcome," the voice says on the audiotape, making me jump.

"Kill that thing, will you?" Taylor snaps.

I click it off and reach into my bag. I wrap my hand around the knife, reminding myself of my mission. I'm here to save Parker. I'm going to find the others.

"Now what?" Taylor asks, as if this is just some random stop on an errand list.

"Now we go in."

"For reals?" Her teeth are clenched. She's itching her palm.

"I mean it," I tell her. "You can turn back. I won't be upset."

"Will you turn back with me?"

"I can't." I shake my head.

"Then how can I?" She takes a deep breath and starts toward the building.

TAYLOR

IT'S JUST AFTER TWO IN THE AFTERNOON, BUT THE sky is gray and the clouds hang low, making it feel much later. We move across the courtyard, passing by a huge water fountain with a basin that looks like an ice cream dish—rounded bottom, tulip top. Behind it, there's a sculpture of a curly-haired boy with a wide-open mouth. His blank eyes angle toward the ominous sky. This whole scene flashes me back to my Gothic horror days—when I was in love with anything Stoker-ish.

I reach out to take Ivy's hand, but she's got it stuffed in her bag. Her inky-dark hair blows back from her face, accentuating her pale (ghostly) skin and rose-colored lips; she reminds me a little of Allison Hayes from *The Undead.*

As we move up the front staircase, there's a tugging sensation inside my gut—one that tells me I should go back. I mean, seriously? The spooky house, the creepy gargoyles, the iron fencing, and the fact that we're in the middle of nowhere without cell phones... "This whole scene has got classic horror doom written all over it."

Ivy remains mute. She hasn't spoken in the last several minutes, and it's starting to freak me out.

The front doors appear to tower over us by at least three feet. Ivy stops a few steps behind me, her eyes hyper-focused, as if they could burn the place down with a single blink.

"Okay, this whole Carrie White routine has got to stop," I tell her. "Say something. I need to know that you haven't been body-snatched."

Finally she takes my hand, and together we inch through the entrance doors. There are hundreds of tiny candles scattered about the lobby area—on the floor, lining the walls.

"Someone's here," I say, stating the obvious.

She takes another step; a broken floor tile crunches beneath her shoe. The ceiling is broken too. There's a hole overhead, where there might've once been a chandelier. Mangled wires hang down from it.

Another eerie sculpture faces us on the back wall. It looks like it was done in limestone: a life-size woman reading a book, with children swooning at her feet. The children look possessed— tiny pupils, darted eyebrows, rounded faces, and dimpled cheeks. Beyond the sculpture is a grand staircase with wide steps and thick banister railings. I picture myself falling through the center, mid-ascent.

"So, maybe this wasn't such a nifty idea." I gaze back at the entrance doors, beyond tempted to bolt.

"What's that?" Ivy asks, nodding to a package at the foot of the sculpture. It's about the size of a shoebox and tied with a big red bow. Beside it is a hefty flashlight.

"A party favor?" I offer, trying to keep things light for the sake of my own sanity. I pick the package up and give it a shake. Something knocks around inside it. "Do you want to do the honors?"

"You can," she says, her hand stuffed inside her bag again.

I look back at the entrance doors once more, picturing myself leaving, trying to formulate an excuse. My fingers fumble as I work to untie the ribbon. I don't get the knot undone on the first few tries.

"Need some help?" Ivy asks.

"I got it," I say, finally pulling the ribbon free. I open the box and peek inside.

At the same moment, the front doors slam shut with a loud,

heavy thud. The box springs from my hands, dropping to the floor.

"No!" I shout, going for the door. The sound of bolts locking echoes inside my brain. My heart tightens into a fist. The handle doesn't budge.

Music starts to play—the theme song to *Haunt Me*.

"Shit, shit, *shit*!" I shout, pounding on the door, knowing I totally blew it.

Tears fill Ivy's eyes. I'm crying too—on the inside, trying to hold it together. I'm so freaking stupid.

"This song," she mutters. "My parents. The killer played this just after . . ." She focuses back on the gift box.

I move to pick it up, revealing what's inside: a video camera— the kind that straps to your head. There are earphones attached, with another piece that curls downward for a mic, reminding me of a 911 operator. "Put it on," I tell her.

"You can't be serious."

"Look," I say, forcing the camera into her hands. "This isn't exactly *my* idea of fun, either. But since you came to play, don't you think you should follow the rules—at least to begin with?"

Ivy reluctantly slips the video camera on so that the lens shoots out from the center of her forehead and the headphones rest over her ears. The tiny voice piece hovers a few inches in front of her mouth.

"There's crackling," she says, signaling to her earphones.

I move closer and grab one of the earpieces to listen.

"Welcome to *my* nightmare, Princess," a voice plays, making my stomach twist.

"Are you ready to be a star?" he asks. "You survived *your* worst nightmare. Now, it's time for you to experience *mine*—a place that haunted me when I was a young boy. The cameras are rolling—except for your camera, that is. And how nice that you brought a co-star. Taylor Monroe, are you ready to reclaim your role?"

"Go screw yourself," I shout into the mic. I take Ivy's hand and give it a firm squeeze. "We're going to get through this," I tell her, trying to convince myself the same. I muster my best smile, pretending to be acting a role, telling myself this isn't real.

I thought *I* was jittery, but Ivy's trembling like a diabetic in need of Pixy Stix. Still, I click on her camera, really wishing I'd gone with my gut.

From the Journal of E.W.

Grade 7, August Preparatory School

WINTER 1972

I woke up to whispering. A boy's voice: "Find it. Get it."

If only I knew what the "it" was.

My mother used to tell me that Johnny's "it" was setting my grandparents' house on fire, just as he had done years before (to his house—the one that had been there before Nana and Gramps built their new one).

I grab my Mary statue. "Why?" I ask it, wishing Mary could explain all the stuff that's been happening: these visions and voices; seeing Ricky's face when I look in the mirror; and spotting him in the library, between stacks of books, with a noose around his neck.

Sometimes I feel like I'm in a movie—like none of this is real. But then I press Mary against my cheek, hard, until my teeth cut the flesh inside my mouth. The blood is real. All of this is real.

Ivy

"I TRUST THAT THE CAMERA IS PROPERLY AFFIXED TO your head." His voice in my ear makes my head feel dizzy. "Now I can see things from your point of view. Do you have any idea how exciting that is to me?"

I bite the inside of my cheek, imagining the camera like a ticking time bomb, about to go off. Taylor stands by my side, listening in, one of the earpieces turned outward.

"This building used to belong to August Prep," the voice continues. "The school opened in 1896. Thomas Shumacher, the owner of this estate, wanted to create a small, multi-aged academic environment that would cater to alternative learning styles and accept boys from all walks of life and with various areas of interest. I lived at this very boarding school, where five years prior to my admission, a student had committed suicide."

"Too bad that student wasn't *you*," Taylor says, speaking to the camera on my head.

"Parents pulled their sons from August as rumors about the suicide spread," the voice continues. "Many believed the building was haunted. By the time I got here, the number of students had dropped from forty-eight to just twelve. Do you believe in hauntings, Princess? Things that go bump in the night?"

"And now for the million-dollar question: Why does he keep calling you Princess?" Taylor asks.

I shake my head. I don't have an answer. There's a prickly sensation all over my skin.

"You'll have just four hours to save the others," the voice says. "In order to do that, you'll need to get through every challenge and follow all of the instructions."

"Every challenge?" I whisper.

"Every challenge has a clue," he explains, as if speaking directly to me. "If you want to find the others, you'll need to collect all of those clues. Now, let's begin. Proceed to room number two."

Taylor hands me the flashlight. She has her own—one of those mini keychain ones. She clicks it on and begins to look around, heading to the area behind the statue. There's a doorway to the right of a grand staircase. She pushes the door open.

We've found the kitchen. It's huge—like for a chef—with high ceilings, stainless-steel appliances, and a crumbling tile floor. Beyond the kitchen is a dining area with long rectangular tables. I angle my flashlight all around and catch something moving out of the corner of my eye.

To my left.

By the fridge.

I shine my flashlight at it, feeling my whole body tense.

"Holy shit," Taylor says, following my gaze.

A boy's face is there, on the fridge door. Blond hair, angry eyes, a scowl across his lips. The image is transparent, as if it's being projected somehow. I turn to look behind me, where there's a wall of cabinets. I open a few of the doors, wondering if there might be a camera hidden inside.

"It's gone," Taylor says.

I swivel back around. The image has vanished. But still I can feel someone's eyes on me. "Let's go," I say, leading us through the dining area.

We take a turn into a hallway. Candles help light the way—wall sconces positioned about five feet apart. I shine my flashlight over cracked walls with peeling paint and insulation peeking through the ceiling.

"Bingo," Taylor says, standing in front of an open door. She angles her flashlight at the number two hung on the wall.

I move to stand beside her, and peek inside the room. More candles light up the space; they're set atop elementary school desks lined up in rows. There's a portable chalkboard at the front of the room. The words WELCOME TO MY NIGHTMARE are scribbled across the surface.

"Remind me why I followed you here," Taylor says. "And why does it smell like rotting fruit?"

I take a step inside. A screen drops down behind the teacher's desk, covering the chalkboard. An old-fashioned film projector at the back of the room, just a few feet away from us, clicks on. The screen goes dark and grainy.

I turn to look at Taylor, just as the classroom door swings shut, nearly smacking her in the face. She jumps back, into the hall. I hear the lock turn.

"Ivy?" she shouts. The doorknob jiggles as she struggles to get back in.

I try the knob too. It doesn't budge. The door is solid wood; there are no windows to smash. My hands wrapped around the knob, I yank with all my might, my foot propped against the wall for added strength.

There's a clamoring sound in the hallway. A moment later, the knob pulls away in my grip. I go soaring back, landing smack against the floor.

"Are you okay?" Taylor asks.

I get up. My back aches. There's a clanking sound against the door on the other side. She's trying to get her knob back into place.

I try as well, aiming my flashlight into the hole; it seems there's a metal bar that I need to fit through a squarish space. After several seconds, I finally get the bar to slide in, but the door still won't open.

"Would you like a cookie?" a voice asks from behind me.

I turn to look. There's a girl on the projector screen. Little Sally Jacobs from Justin Blake's Night Terrors films. I recognize her right away: her dark red braids, her purple sundress, the skeleton keys jammed into her eyes.

She's holding a tray full of cookies. "This batch just came out of the oven." She smiles wide, despite the blood running down her cheeks. "I also have fresh lemonade inside my house. Want to come have a glass?"

The movie projector makes a click-click-clicking sound. Meanwhile, it's quiet out in the hallway now. I place my ear up against the door. "Taylor? Are you still out there?"

"*Hellooooo*," Little Sally Jacobs sings. "I believe I asked you a

question. Cat got your tongue? Or maybe *I've* got the cat's tongue."
She giggles, pulling a short red tongue from behind her ear like
a coin trick. The tongue wiggles between her fingers. She pops it
into her mouth and swallows it down like candy. "*Yummy, yummy
in my tummy,*" she sings.

"Taylor?" I call again, knocking on the door.

The image of Little Sally Jacobs darkens on the screen. The
background behind her grays as well. It looks as if she's hidden
in shadows. I can no longer see her face or features, nor can I tell
that her dress is purple.

By the time the image lightens, it's morphed into a woman—
someone much older than Little Sally Jacobs. Wearing a long
black dress, the woman has her hair pulled back into a tight bun
atop her head, and there are deep lines in her face.

"You're a naughty, naughty girl," she hisses. The lines in her
face seem to deepen and multiply as she moves closer and her
image becomes bigger. It looks as if she's moving out from the
screen, as if this footage is three-dimensional.

She points at me, her finger waggling left and right, scolding
me, forbidding me.

"Taylor?" I shout again, unable to recognize the woman. She
isn't from one of Justin Blake's films.

"Go stand in the corner," she snaps.

I bite the inside of my cheek, waiting for the moment to pass.

"You heard me," she continues, moving into the center of the room, as if the image has morphed again, become a three-dimensional hologram. "As a student here at August Prep, you will do as you are told. Now, if you don't go stand in the corner, you won't ever get to see your friends. Is that what you really want?"

My mind starts to race. By *friends*, does she mean the other contest winners? Does it include Taylor too?

The woman has a cookie now. "*Mmmm*," she says, moaning over its goodness. A trickle of blood drools out her mouth and rolls down her chin. There's an eerie grin on her face. "Oatmeal-raisin. Would you like a bite?"

I brush Parker's T-shirt bracelet against my cheek, reminding myself why I'm here.

She grimaces when I don't answer. Her eyes narrow into slits. "I'll tell you one final time," she says; her teeth are stained with red. "Get in the corner—*now!*"

I do as she says, moving to the far corner of the room, reassuring myself that there are still more challenges to tackle, more scenes in his movie. The killer's going to play with me for a while.

"Ivy?" Another voice.

I turn to look.

Natalie's there, on the screen. The hologram is gone.

"Where are you?" she asks, looking all around as if trying to find me.

My heart beats harder. My pulse races faster. Was this prerecorded? Or is it possible that it's live, that she knows I'm here?

Her wig is off. Her hair's uneven—shorter in some places, longer in others. She's wearing the same clothes from the Dark House amusement park night—the layers of black and gray.

"You're probably wondering how I'm still alive," she says. "I saw the rough-cut version of the film. It looked like I died, didn't it? Like a giant piece of pointed glass fell on top of my head. But I was able to step back, thanks to Harris's warning, just in time. The glass landed on my foot—my leg, actually—right above my boot laces, hitting an artery." Staring straight into the camera, she kicks her foot out from beneath her dress. Her leg's been wrapped with a bandage. "There was a lot of blood, Ivy. I hope you never had to see it. Lucky for me, our elfin friend doubles as a medic."

Her face looks exactly as I remember it, if not a bit thinner: pale blue eyes, pointed chin, dark full lips. The background behind her has been blacked out, so I can't see where she is.

"My clue for you is April showers. Now, can you guess where you need to go next? I'll give you a little hint." She reaches into the pocket of her dress and takes out a tiny book. "*Shhhh,*" she hushes, placing her finger up to her lips. "There's no talking in here." She opens the book up to the middle and begins to read.

I nod, suspecting I know the answer to her clue.

"Oh, and before I forget," she says, moving closer to the camera, as if about to let me in on a secret. "If you're seeing this video, then you know that Harris has been right all along. He was right about the amusement park, wasn't he? And about your fear of being videotaped? So, know that he'll be right about this."

Huh?

"He has a warning for you too," she insists. "Don't let her out—"

Static cuts off her words, filling the room with an ear-deafening hum. I remain staring at the screen, not wanting to move, desperate for her to reappear.

But she doesn't.

And I can't—move, that is. My chest tightens. My head feels even dizzier than before. I clench my teeth and hold my breath, while the room starts to spin. I silently count to ten, waiting for the sensation to pass, remembering something that Dr. Donna used to say: "The physical side effects of the emotions that we feel... those are as temporary as the emotions themselves."

After a few moments, I'm able to squat down to the floor. I lower my head between my knees, hoping the rush of blood to my brain will give me a surge of stability and enable me to breathe normally.

"Ivy?" Another voice.

I can hear again. The hum has stopped. I lift my head—the room wobbles into place—and peer over my shoulder.

Taylor is standing by the projector. There's a remote control in her hand. "Are you okay?"

The door is open again. Both knobs are in place.

"I went to look for something to wedge into the door crack," she tries to explain. "But I couldn't find anything, and so I gave the knob another shot. Wait, are you okay?" Her face scrunches at the sight of me.

I can feel the panic all over my body—a cold, tingling sensation. But there's another sensation too. Hope? Gratitude? Is there a word that falls in between?

Because Natalie's still alive.

There isn't doubt in my mind now.

IVY FILLS ME IN ON WHAT HAPPENED, LOOKING ALL
around as she does—into the hallway, at the projector screen, over
both shoulders, and in the far corner.

"Natalie's alive," she says. "It was her, on the screen. April
showers."

"Okay, my head hurts."

"That's the clue. Natalie said it." Instead of shedding any additional light, Ivy moves out into the hallway, ever eager for more
punishment.

I begin to follow, just as a door slams shut somewhere, freezing me in place. There's a sound of footsteps—wooden heels against marble floor tiles. I can't tell which direction it's coming from. I look back toward the classroom, and then down the hallway. A few moments later the footsteps stop, but still my heart keeps pounding.

"There," Ivy says, spotting a sign for the library. It points us just a few doors down. "That's where Natalie said we need to go."

I follow Ivy inside, immediately struck by what I see. The names of all the contest winners (FRANKIE, PARKER, NATALIE, GARTH, SHAYLA, IVY, and TAYLOR) are splattered across the walls in dark-red paint. There are portraits of all of us too, done in a Renaissance style with rich colors and serious expressions.

While Ivy moves toward the portrait of Parker, I check out the one of Garth. His dark eyes are mesmerizing; I can almost feel them somehow, watching me, studying my every move.

The library is about the size of a gymnasium, with super-high ceilings and a monster fireplace that's big enough to stand in. There's a main circulation desk at the front, a baby grand piano at the back, a bunch of study tables in between, as well as rows and rows of books.

Ivy and I move to the reference desk—a thick mahogany island littered with the dust of broken tile. I aim my flashlight at the ceiling, where there's a hand-painted scene of seven sad-looking children sitting in a circle, all holding the same book. "Creepy super freaky," I mutter, also noticing a three-tiered chandelier.

Ivy searches the desk, in hopes of finding another clue perhaps. "There's crackling again," she says, placing her hands on the headset.

I move closer to listen, bracing myself to hear his voice.

"Welcome to the library, Princess," he says. "The smell of fine literature lingers in the air, doesn't it? The notes of vanilla and nutmeg? The acidic scent that comes with paper and ink. Ricky Slater used to escape in here to read the greats: Hemingway, Poe, Keats, Proust... you name it. One thing most people don't know about Ricky, however, is that it was the voice in his head that he was really trying to escape—the one that told him how inadequate he was: socially defunct, unable to relate to those around him, even on those rare occasions that he tried. The reason *I* know all of this... as you can imagine, Ricky was a hot topic after his fatal departure, not to mention that I'm the one who found his suicide note—stuck in the pages of *Madame Bovary*, his most checked-out work. I want you to go find the note now."

Ivy stares at me, her mouth snarled open, as if there's a booger hanging out my nose.

"*What?*" I sniff.

"Do you believe in ghosts?"

"Well, *duh*. Ever see *The Amityville Horror* or *The Conjuring?* I don't mess with spirit shit."

As if on cue, music starts to play from an old-fashioned record player in the corner.

I go to check it out. It's one of those big, boxy players with the automatic arm and the vinyl disk that goes round and round.

A female voice sings: *"I've got my eye on youuuuuu, Sweet Cherry Pie. My eye's on youuuuuu, oh, no, I can't deny. Oh, Baby Boooooo, I'll be coming for youuuuuu."* Denise Kilborn's voice; she's one of my dad's favorite singers.

The rhythm is slow and haunting. It's being played at the wrong speed. There's a lever at the top of the player. I move it a notch to fix the speed, but nothing happens. I click the power off, but still the machine plays—even when I smack the arm off the record, scratching the needle across the vinyl. The music is obviously coming from somewhere else.

I shine my flashlight all around, searching for a speaker. Instead I find two glowing red lights, two aisles over, in the stacks of books. The lights hover over a set of encyclopedias.

I move closer, angling my flashlight between the bookshelves, able to see that the lights are actually eyes.

They belong to a boy—the same one we saw in the kitchen, against the door of the fridge.

Ivy screams at the sight of him—a bloodcurdling wail.

I move to the end of his aisle. The boy looks freakishly real. He has a stark white face and blond hair, and is dressed in prep-school gear: khaki pants, navy suit jacket, leather loafers, striped tie. He's standing against the wall, staring in my direction.

I get even closer; I'm just a few inches away now. He looks about fourteen years old.

"Taylor?" Ivy's voice. She's standing behind me, at the end of the aisle.

There's a pile of books at the boy's feet and something metal gripped in his hand. He grabs a book off the shelf, opens it up, and plunges down with the metal object: a librarian's due-date stamp. The word DIE! appears on the inside cover.

He tosses the book, grabs another, and does the same; his teeth clench with the force of his stamping.

DIE!

DIE!

DIE!

He goes to take yet another book—a copy of *The Masque of the Red Death*, by Edgar Allan Poe. But instead of stamping, he pauses. His eyes zoom in my direction again, as if he can really see me.

The music stops. The boy's lips part. He's mouthing something, but I can't hear him.

"What?" I move closer.

"Get out," he hisses. A deep, angry voice.

A shiver runs down my spine. I take a step back, bumping into Ivy, letting out a gasp.

She pulls me away, her fingernails digging into my skin as she brings me back to the main area, with all the study tables. "Did you blow out some of the candles?" she asks me.

It takes my brain a beat to make sense of the question—to notice that while most of the candles in the library remain lit, the ones on the study tables have all been blown out. Tendrils of smoke linger in the air, as does the smell of sulfur.

"No." I shake my head.

"Someone's been here. With us."

No shit, Sherlock.

Her flashlight stops on a sign at the end of a row of stacks, denoting the call numbers of the books contained within.

"The Dewey Dummy Decimal System." I sigh. "Some evil librarian's idea of classification." I angle my flashlight over the card catalog—basically a hutchlike piece of furniture with a bunch of narrow drawers containing a bazillion tiny index cards. "Lucky for you I used to volunteer at my school library. The ball-busting, menthol-smelling librarian insisted that I learn Dewey, the old-school way." I open up the appropriate drawer, and sift through the row of cards, eventually finding the right one. "Gustave Flaubert's *Madame Bovary*," I announce, pulling the card out. "Eight-forty-three-point-eight." I move my flashlight beam over the series of call numbers at the ends of the rows of stacks, finally landing on the right one. "Bingo," I say.

Ivy takes the card and hurries in that direction—a couple of rows over from the DIE!-stamping boy. She squats down at the end of the aisle, running her fingers over torn, cracked spines.

"It's here," she says, after only a few moments. *Madame Bovary* looks absolutely ancient with its wrinkled yellow pages, most of which are loose. Ivy flips through it, her hands trembling.

"Hurry up," I tell her, more than anxious to move on.

"Shhh," a voice says from behind, making me jump.

Ivy jumps too, and lets out a gasp.

An old woman is there, behind us, wearing a billowy white dress. She has long gray hair and the most wrinkled skin I've ever seen; the lines form tiny checkerboards. "Are you ready to check out?" she asks, her eyes rolled up toward the ceiling.

Ivy's in complete panic mode. She avoids the librarian's gaze, continuing to search for the note. But I remain looking at the woman—at the dark-red tears running down her face, getting caught up in those checkerboard lines.

The old woman's image wavers slightly, but just like the boy, she looks so real.

"I've got it," Ivy says. Her fingers tremble as she opens a folded up piece of paper.

The note has yellowed with age, but the words are still very clear.

Dear Reader:

I'm sorry for what I've done, but I couldn't bear listening to the voices anymore. They creep up on me in the middle of the night and sneak beneath my bedcovers to whisper into my ear. They remind me how foolish I am: foolish for waking up in the morning; foolish for going through the motions of the day; foolish for going to bed at night, only to repeat it all over again.

I'm haunted by other voices too: my parents, teachers, class-mates, dorm monitors, the headmaster. Everybody telling me how I should act, should speak, should feel, should do in school.

"You should read this, not that."

"You should look up, not down."

"You should study harder, not longer."

"You should speak loudly and clearly."

"You should think twice before speaking at all."

My life is an endless black tunnel of "should." But what no one seems to realize is that I hate myself even more than they do, and that the voices in my head are the loudest ones of all. This is the only way I know how to silence them—this is my "should."

Love,
Ricky

"Holy shit," Ivy whispers.

"What's the clue?" I ask her.

Ivy looks back down at the letter, and then at the bookshelf.

"Are you ready to check out?" the old lady asks again. She starts to laugh—a high-pitched cackle.

Ivy drops the book. Pages spill out onto the floor.

I pick them up, along with the book, and flip the cover open to the front—to the spot where the checkout card goes. Ricky's name is there, on the card. "He signed the book out a bunch of times, which either means he was a really slow reader..."

"*Or?*" Ivy asks, champing at the proverbial bit.

"Or he was just really into horny, middle-aged French chicks."

"This isn't funny."

"Who's laughing? Beside Grandma Creepy, that is." I nod to the old lady. "Look," I say, doing a doubletake at the checkout card. "Beside Ricky's name... It says twenty-eight R."

She holds the card super close to her face, like an old man with cataracts. "It has to be a clue."

"Okay, but what does it mean? And how does it go with April showers?"

"April's my real name," she says.

"Since when?"

"Since before it had to be changed."

"Okay," I say, for lack of better words, assuming the name change

212

must have something to do with her parents' murder. "And...
you take a lot of showers?"

Before she can comment, the music starts up again: "*I've got my
eye on you, Sweet Honey Bee. My eye's on you. There ain't no leavin'
me. With me, you'll be, for all eternity.*"

"Ugh," I moan, barely able to think straight, let alone crack
the all-important code.

As we start toward the door, I hear something else—a turbulent clamor that stops us in our tracks, like metal tearing through
metal. I cover my ears and look around, trying to figure out where
the sound is coming from. A dusting of cement sprinkles down
on top of our heads.

I look upward. The chandelier wobbles from side to side. I
push Ivy out of the way just as it comes soaring down, crashing
into a table, snapping it in two.

Ivy lets out another enviable scream, and we both hurry out of
the library, my heart hammering, my nerves shot. And still that
creepy Denise Kilborn music plays in the background.

NATALIE SORRENTO

HARRIS SAYS THAT I'VE BEEN HERE FOR MONTHS now, but I wouldn't be surprised if it's been closer to a year. I've lost track of time.

I'm cold, hungry. My bones ache. My muscles twitch.

Is Ivy really going to come?

Facing the wall, I tell myself that this isn't really a prison cell, that I merely climbed down inside a manhole and found myself a nice little alcove where I could be alone. *Being here is my choice*, I repeat inside my head. *Nobody made me come. Nothing's making me stay. I can leave whenever I want.* I grab a few strands of hair—nice long ones with lots of elastic. I give them a quick tug. The follicles look like snow.

I wonder what my parents are thinking, what the news is saying, if anyone cares. I can almost hear my parents now:

My mother: *"We tried to steer our daughter in the right direction, but she never would listen."*

My father: *"She was too obsessed with this Justin Blake person. Someone should hold him at least partially responsible for creating such cultish filth."*

Harris says that some of the contest winners are dead. I know I should believe him, but he could also just be saying that so I'll work harder at trying to get out.

There's a clank sound in the distance—metal against metal. He's back. The Nightmare Elf. He wears the suit from the movie, like some deranged fan, giving a bad name to all of Blake's true fans—like me.

The air down here is musty. The smell must be from all the storm drains, I tell myself, picturing a manhole cover, imagining myself lifting it off and climbing down a ladder.

I wind my finger around a clump of hair. More follicle snowflakes sprinkle down in the light. Christmas will be coming soon.

The Elf is getting closer: the sound of footsteps against the cement. I lie down and shut my eyes, so he'll think I've been good and taken all my pills. Hopefully he'll leave me a tasty present.

IVY

BACK IN THE LOBBY, I TRY TO CATCH MY BREATH, silently acknowledging what just happened: a crystal chandelier—so huge and heavy that it was able to break a table in two—almost landed on my head. And if it hadn't been for Taylor pushing me out of the way, it most definitely would have.

"Thanks for saving my life," I tell her.

She's sitting with her back up against the wall. Her head is in her hands. She doesn't look up.

"I'm sorry." I sit down across from her. "I never should've gotten you involved in all of this."

"It's not your fault." She peeks up in my direction. "I was the wise one who followed you here, remember?"

"But only after I showed up at your dorm, in the middle of the night, like an escaped mental patient," I say, remembering her words, as well as the pill container in my bag. I haven't taken my meds in the past couple of days.

"You're *not* really an escaped mental patient, are you?" There's humor in her voice, and yet her expression remains serious.

"No. They let me out for real—on the condition that I take my meds, do as I'm told, go to therapy, and stop trying to set myself on fire."

"*Seriously?*" Her eyeballs bulge.

"Kidding." The joke feels foreign in my mouth; I can't remember the last time I tried to be funny.

"Well, this is way more fun than, say, lounging around in bed or going to the mall."

"Now *you're* joking," I say.

"About hanging out in a creepy, abandoned building and being terrorized by a psycho serial killer trumping such activities as shopping and/or lounging ... you're right; I *am* joking. But I wouldn't want you to go through this alone."

I hold her gaze a moment, wishing that, like the way I felt about Parker, I'd have met her someplace else, under difference circumstances, and that we'd have had a completely normal shopping/

lounging/stay-up-all-night-pigging-out-on-junkfood-and-talking-about-boys kind of friendship.

Instead of this.

I run my fingers over the copy of *Madame Bovary*; the suicide note sticks out between the pages. I read it a few more times, looking for some hidden message. But I don't find anything that goes deeper than the words themselves. "I wonder if any of this is even real."

"What do you mean? Which part?"

"All of it: the suicide note, the story of Ricky, the killer's nightmare, his going to school here..."

"Or if this is just a movie location, you mean? With us as the actors." Taylor looks directly at my strap-on camera and gives it the finger.

I gaze back down at the book and flip to the checkout card. The clue is written in black marker, just like the note itself. "Twenty-eight R."

"*R*, as in right," Taylor guesses. "Like part of a locker combination."

"I guess only time will tell." I fish my notebook out of my bag and open up to a fresh page. I scribble down both of the clues, as well as the phrasing "Don't let her out..."

...of my sight?

... of my mind?

... of this building?

... of my life?

Was Natalie/Harris referring to Taylor? Or Shayla? Or someone else?

There's a clicking sound coming from my headphones. "He's going to say something." I signal to Taylor.

She slides over to join me.

"Enjoying your time so far?" his voice pumps out. "Ticktock, ticktock. Need I remind you that your time is limited?"

Taylor gives my video camera the finger again and then flashes me her watch. We've already burned an hour.

"I was in the seventh grade when I found Ricky's note," the killer says. "People had associated Ricky with *Madame Bovary*, since he'd always had the book in his possession, checked out seventeen times over his two-year stint at August. One might've thought he'd have gotten himself his own personal copy. But, in some way, Ricky liked the attention that came with always checking out the same book—a book about a cheating woman who took her own life, not so much unlike his own mother. At least that's how the rumor went. Alas, Ricky thought that his choice for the note's hiding spot was somewhat poetic, but instead it just proved futile, because no one ever thought to look there. A more obvious spot would have been someplace in his dorm room, left out in the open for all to see. I want you to fix his poor decision now. Find room F and place the note on his bedside table. Then turn off the lights and blow out the candles."

Ivy

WE MOVE PAST THE LOBBY, IN THE OPPOSITE DIRECTION
from the library. There's a long, narrow hallway with broken floor
tiles and rotted moldings. I shine my flashlight along the walls,
startled to find a series of photos taped to the crumbling plaster.

I angle my flashlight closer, feeling my heart pummel. "This
can't be real."

"What can't?" Taylor asks. She's farther down the hallway now.

The photos look brand-new, printed on bright white paper,
with vibrant colors. I focus in on one of the photos. "It's him," I
say, thinking aloud.

The clothes he's wearing are the same...all the layers of charcoal and gray. His hair is the same too: dark and straggly, held back with a bandanna. The photo was taken here. He's sitting on a bench with the courtyard fountain behind him.

"And I repeat: *What can't be real?*" Taylor asks, standing by my side again.

"It's Garth," I say, noticing the sharpness of his jaw.

She moves within kiss distance of the photo. "How can you tell? He's angled away from us. And, wait, where are his hands?"

"It looks like he's got them behind his back," I say, wishing that I could see them too—to recognize any of his silver jewelry. "See there, the way his shoulders protrude outward in an unnatural position. He could be tied up or handcuffed."

I shine my flashlight over the other photos. There's one of Shayla in the lobby, sitting against the wall. Though she's also positioned partially away from the camera, I'm able to spot the pursing of her lips and the flare of her nostrils; it looks like she might be crying.

The photo of Frankie is less clear. It was taken in the library, where he's seated at the piano. His hair has grown out over his eyes. His fingers look mangled and cut up. There's a scar across the front of his wrist. Was it always there? Do I remember it from before?

"Do you think this might be some sort of trick or illusion?" Taylor asks.

I close my eyes and flashback to the Nightmare Elf's video—the one that Parker and I were forced to watch before trying to exit the amusement park. It looked like Frankie had been buried alive. But in the back of my mind I've wondered, hoped: What if the burial was just a scene created for the Nightmare Elf's movie? What if Frankie was dug up and then revived immediately after the scene cut?

Is it possible that Shayla was never really killed? That the Nightmare Elf didn't choke her to death? Maybe he only choked her unconscious.

And what about Garth? Is it such a stretch to think he might've survived having fallen out the window? In the video, there was a close-up shot of an ax, but we never actually saw it come down on Garth.

I've been racking my mind for months, asking myself why the Nightmare Elf would've cut the scenes where he did—why he wouldn't have shown the characters' very last breaths. "They're here. Alive somewhere. Parker is too," I say, thinking about the box of letters in my bag.

"I just don't want you to be disappointed."

"They're here," I repeat, turning away to study the photos

again. Shayla's wearing a pair of gray sweatpants and a big, bulky coat. Frankie's in a hooded sweatshirt; I can't see his legs. Neither of them is in the same clothes as on the night of the Dark House amusement park.

"Okay, but what if these photos were Photoshopped. Wasn't Frankie buried alive at the amusement park?"

"They never found his body," I remind her. "It'd been dug up. No one ever found any bodies."

"Okay, but didn't Garth fall like a kagillion stories out of a building?"

"Who knows how many stories it really was. The camera can and does lie."

"My point exactly."

I clench my teeth. Her words have blades.

"I'm sorry," she says, reaching out to touch my arm. "I can be an insensitive beetle sometimes. I guess I'm just preparing myself for the worst. That's sort of how I deal."

I take a deep breath, and suck up any tears. It's not like I haven't heard these doubts before—from police and people at the hospital, and even from Apple and Core.

Taylor wraps her arm around me. "Don't listen to anything I say. I wasn't even there. I was a coward, remember? I didn't get to meet the others."

"You met Natalie," I say, correcting her.

"Right. And why isn't her picture here? Or Parker's?"

I search the wall, as well as the photos, really wishing I had a clue.

"Look," Taylor begins again, "if you really believe that the people in these photos are the genuine, bona fide players, then I believe you."

"Except they aren't players." I turn to face her again. "They're people."

"Right, and *I'm* an insensitive beetle, remember?"

"If that were true, you wouldn't be here."

"Okay, so maybe only the beetle part is true. I mean, seriously? If someone like you can be so optimistic despite everything she's been through, then what the hell is my problem?"

"Let's just keep moving," I say. "Ticktock, remember?"

We continue down the hallway, passing by classrooms to the left and right. There's a door at the end of the hall. We go through it. Facing us is a mahogany stairwell that leads up and down.

"Should we try the basement?" I ask.

"Do you really think that prep school kids would agree to sleeping by leaky water pipes and mousetraps?"

"Maybe not."

"Now, if *I* were a dorm room..." Taylor taps her chin in thought. "Upstairs?"

"It's worth a try."

We hike up the stairs, two at a time. At the top there's another long hallway. Sheets of paper are sprinkled about the floor—fresh paper, the texture is crisp, the color is bright white. I trample over a couple of sheets before picking one up.

"What is it?" Taylor asks.

"'In a thousand words or less,'" I read aloud, "'describe your worst nightmare. By Jenna Adams.'"

"*Huh?*"

"They're contest entries," I say, shining my flashlight over pages and pages of nightmares—there has to be over a hundred of them. "Some of the people who didn't win, maybe."

Taylor nods, reading one of them. "This person dreams about the chicken in her freezer coming to life in the middle of the night and paying her back by pecking at her face."

"Except if it's frozen chicken, then its beak's been removed."

"Not necessarily." She grimaces.

While Taylor proceeds down the hallway, I poke my head into a few of the rooms. You can tell that the core of this building was probably once a mansion. Though set up with school desks and chairs, most of the rooms have hardwood floors, ornate pillars, and sculptured fireplaces.

I step inside an office, noticing a shiny red apple sitting in the middle of an ink blotter. I point my flashlight at it, trying to see if the apple's real. I pick it up. It's definitely real. I puncture the skin with my fingernail; the juice pulls away on my thumb. I go to put the apple back.

And that's when I notice.

The ink blotter is actually a calendar. It's set to April 1966. There's an illustration of storm clouds and rain droplets decorating the April heading.

"April showers," I whisper, flipping the page to May. Daisies and daffodils frame the page. *Bring May flowers.*

A giant *X* is marked over May 9th.

"Will you help me?" a male voice whispers, from behind, making me jump.

I turn to look.

A girl with swollen dark eyes stares back at me. Her lips are chapped. Her cheeks look sallow and sunken.

I take a step closer, suddenly realizing that the girl is me—my reflection, my ghostly appearance, my ratty hair. I'm looking in a full-length mirror. The words SAVE THE DATE are scribbled across my image. I reach out to touch one of the letters. A smear of red comes away on my finger.

"Knock, knock." Another voice. It steals my breath, even though I recognize it right away.

I open the door.

Taylor's standing there. "What gives?" she asks. "And why do you look all Laurie Strode?"

"Laurie *who?*"

She rolls her eyes. "From *Halloween* . . . Jamie Lee Curtis's character. She always looked so haunted." Taylor continues to ramble on about some bedroom scene and the boogeyman.

I'm only half paying attention, trying to listen for that male voice—the one that asked for help.

"So, do you want to find room F or what?" Taylor asks.

I nod and move back into the hall, slamming the door behind me.

From the Journal of E.W.

Grade 7, August Preparatory School

WINTER 1972

"You'll die in here too," a voice whispered, over and over, eventually waking me up.

It was Ricky's voice, hours ago. I shot up in bed.

Ricky's face stared back at me in the window glass.

I blinked and rubbed my eyes, but the image of him wouldn't go away.

I got up and went to the door, turned the lock, and tried to get out. But the knob wouldn't turn, even when I moved the lock left and right.

I pounded on the door, flashing back to being locked in my room years before. "Somebody get me out of here!" I shouted, glancing back at the window. Ricky was smirking now.

Mother had been like that too.

Finally, Mr. Shunter came. He opened the door without a problem. By that point, Ricky had vanished.

"Can I sleep in your room?" I asked him. "I'll bring my blanket and pillow. I can sleep right on the floor."

"Go back to bed, Ethan," he said, turning away and going back down the hall.

I've been under the covers since, adding to my prayer cards. Here are a couple that I've been working on:

RICKY, GO AWAY

This is my fortress.
You can't touch me here.

Protection is all around me.
Within these walls, I have no fear.

The guardians are watching down.
The gods are listening in.

Go away, go away,
For you will never win.

YOUR MISERY EVER AFTER

You made your choice.
I can make mine.

Might as well stop haunting.
In my fortress, I'm divine.

I may never rest.
But you will never sleep.

How is that for irony?
A life in Limbo you will reap.

IVY

"WE NEED TO FIND ANOTHER PART OF THE BUILD-
ing," Taylor says, pointing toward the room numbers. "Nine, ten,
eleven, fourteen…"

I nod. She's right. "We need to find the lettered rooms."

We move down the hall. A sign for the dormitory points us
back downstairs. On the first floor again, I notice a door to the
left without a room number over it. I open it wide.

This isn't a classroom or an office. There's a narrow hallway
with a low ceiling and a ramp that leads downward. "Come on,"
I say, wishing my flashlight beam were brighter.

The dormitory must've been added on. I picture us moving through a tunnel, into another building altogether.

"Talk about a claustrophobic's worst nightmare," Taylor says.

I'd have to agree. There are no doors or windows, and there's barely enough room for two people to pass through, headed in opposite directions.

"Where are you going?" a male voice stutters out.

I stop. And look back. Taylor shines her flashlight all around. But we don't see anything. There doesn't appear to be anyone.

We continue through the tunnel. The sound of footsteps follows us.

"I wouldn't go in there if I were you," the same voice whispers.

Someone screams. A female voice. A piercing blare that burrows into my heart.

I stop again. Taylor's right behind me. "Who was that?" I ask, my mind zooming to Natalie and Shayla.

Taylor shakes her head.

I turn back around, finally reaching the other side of the tunnel. There's a pocket door. I slide it open and then slam it closed behind us, trying to catch my breath.

There's a staircase that leads upward and a crude cement hallway—cracked floors, visible overhead pipes—that goes to the right.

Taylor shines her flashlight over a sign by the stairwell,

welcoming us to the dormitory and pointing us upstairs. "Jackpot," she says.

My adrenaline pumps as I move up the steps, finally reaching the top. There's another narrow space. A long skinny hallway. I search the room numbers. They're in alphabetical order.

The door to room B is open. There are two single beds, two dressers, and a small corner desk. Like the rest of the place, the windows have been boarded up.

"Room F," Taylor says. She's moved down the hall, standing outside the room.

"Welcome to the dormitory, Princess." The killer's voice is a soft purr; it stops me in my tracks. "Nice work finding Ricky's room. I made up the bed, especially for you. But don't get too comfortable yet. Don't forget about Ricky's note."

"Is he talking to you right now?" Taylor asks.

I nod, moving forward again. I stand by Taylor's side to peek inside the room. There are spotlights over the bed and on the desk illuminating the space. There are also candles lit on the dresser, several more on an overhead shelf, and a bunch of tiny ones on the windowsills.

"What's he saying?" Taylor asks, grabbing an earpiece to listen.

"Be sure to blow out all the candles before you lay down to sleep," the voice continues. "And turn off all the lights, including flashlights. It's important that things are completely dark for shut-eye, wouldn't you agree? Lastly, I'll need you to close the door, leaving Taylor outside. Do all of that now."

Taylor shoves her hand over the camera lens. With her other hand, she blocks the mic to muffle our voices. "Don't close the door," she whispers. "It's not like he'll know."

"Have you not noticed the thing on my head that you're currently blocking? It's not exactly a tiara."

"So, what if you close the door and then I'll wait a few seconds and open it back up? If you're laying down, your camera's focus will be at the ceiling. And even if there are other cameras, the focus is going to be on you."

"Okay," I nod, more than anxious to get this over with. I close the door behind me and move into the room.

I unfold the note and set it on the bedside table, beside a book with gold trim. If only Ricky had done the same years ago, maybe people would've found his note. Maybe it would've become public. Maybe we wouldn't be here right now.

"Everything okay?" Taylor shouts.

"Just dandy," I mutter, shining my flashlight all around. The inside of the room looks a lot like the first one I looked at, with the exception of two beds; this room is a single.

"Ivy?" Taylor shouts again. The knob jiggles back and forth. She can't get the door to open.

My heart tightens. The room starts to tilt. I move back to the door. "The knob won't turn." I try to twist it, pull it, and wrench it with all my might. But nothing makes a difference. The door won't open.

I take a step back, wondering if the killer's here somewhere, in this room, under the bed. Could he be using a remote control? I try to maintain normal breath, but it gets caught in my lungs. I press my forehead against the door and silently count to ten.

"Do you want me to go look for something to break the lock?" Taylor asks. "Or I can stay right here and talk to you the whole time. Just tell me whatever's best."

There's a broken-glass sensation inside my chest. I look toward the bottom of the bed and scoot down, shining my flashlight beneath it. But I don't see anything.

"Ivy?" Taylor calls.

"I'll be fine," I call back, suspecting what this is about. The door won't open until the killer gets this scene.

I blow out all the candles and click off both spotlights. Sitting down on the edge of the bed, I close my eyes, preparing myself for the darkness. I breathe in the scent of the blown-out candles, trying to think of happier times, like my purple birthday cake two years ago and the wish I made for someone like Parker to come into my life.

I run my lips over his T-shirt bracelet, imagining that it still smells like him—a musky, salty scent. I click off my flashlight and open my eyes, almost unable to believe what I see.

There are numbers scribbled across the wall: 843.8, the call number for *Madame Bovary*. The digits glow in the dark. They're written all over—again and again and again—in different sizes, without spaces: 843.8843.8843.8843.8843.8843.8843.8843.8843.8...

Beneath a heading that reads BE CAREFUL WHAT YOU DREAM are the images that represent the nightmares of all of us contest winners: an eel (Parker), an ax (Garth), a bear (Taylor), a tombstone (Frankie), a broken mirror (Natalie), a noose (Shayla), and a pair of demon eyes (me).

There are more images too: a carousel with a possessed horse, and a boy and a girl holding hands at the entrance gate to an amusement park, separated by bars.

"Ivy?" Taylor shouts.

"Hurry up now, Princess. Be a good girl and get into bed."

My teeth clenched, I peel back the covers. There are glow-in-the-dark words there too, scribbled across the sheet. *Ricky was here, but now he's dead. Nobody ever listened to a word he said.*

I wheeze—an air-sucking noise that doesn't sound human.

"Ivy?" Taylor's pounding on the door now. "Say something. Tell me you're okay."

"I'm fine," I try to shout, but the words are barely audible.

"Are you all snuggled up now, Princess? Snug as a bug in a rug?"

I lie down and reach for my flashlight, just to know that it's there. But I can't seem to find it now.

"If you haven't already guessed it, this was my room as well. I was the first student at August to be assigned to room F after Ricky. And so I slept in Ricky's bed, wrote in my diary at Ricky's desk, put my clothes away in his drawers, walked in his same path."

My mind zeroes in on the book on the night table. Could that be the diary he's talking about?

"It wasn't long before I became haunted by Ricky," his voice continues. "All because he wanted me to find his note. I'd wake up to the sound of Ricky whispering in my ear: *843.8, help me, find it.* I started to see flashes of that number everywhere: in class, on the radio, in phone numbers and zip codes. I'd look at the mirror and it'd be scrawled across the shower steam. Then I'd blink and it'd be gone. Imagine what that was like for me, Princess—for a twelve-year-old boy to try to make sense of that madness: *843.8*," he whispers. *"Help me, find it. 843.8, help me, find it. 843.8, help me, find it. 843.8, help me, find it . . ."*

"Hello?" Another voice; it calls out over his whispering.

I sit up, like a reflex, and rake my fingers over the bedcovers, still trying to find the flashlight.

"Are you there?" the voice asks.

Shayla?

It sounds like it's coming from somewhere behind me or under the bed.

"Come out, come out, wherever you are!" a voice sings.

"Garth?" I climb out of the bed and get down on my hands and knees. I reach beneath the bed—as far as I can stretch—picturing a scene in one of the Nightmare Elf movies, when Annie's Chatty Cathy doll comes to life, hides in the middle of the night, and stabs Annie's searching hand with a pair of scissors.

"Hello?" Shayla says again.

I crawl out and squat down by the bedpost. There's glowing writing on the wall: 36 L. I touch the spot, running my fingers over a series of slats. This must be a heating vent. "Shayla?" I call, suspecting her voice is coming from the other side of it. "Can you hear me? Is Garth there too?"

"I'm downstairs," she says.

"*Where* downstairs?"

"Come out here and I'll tell you."

"What? Out *where*?"

A knocking sound comes from the other side of the room—against the wall, by the door; a hard, frantic pounding.

"Taylor?" I shout, wondering if the sound is from her.

"Your role has been cut, Ms. Belmont," the Nightmare Elf says, his voice coming from the heating vent.

A motor revs, making it hard to hear anything else. I recognize the sound. A chain saw. Like in *Nightmare Elf*. It's coming from the vent as well.

Shayla lets out a scream—a thick, throaty wail that rivals the rev of the motor and slices through my chest. *"No!"* she screams.

A few moments later, the chain saw motor stops.

"Shayla?" I place my ear against the vent, desperate to hear even a breath. Instead, I hear music.

Instrumentals.

Song lyrics.

A woman's voice.

An old tune from an old movie: *"Baby, can I play for you? I'll dance and sing and play for you. Just pull my puppet strings, and I'll do anything. Oh, Baby, I can play for you."*

My nostrils flare. My lips bunch. A hand touches me from behind.

Taylor's hand.

Her familiar face.

I can see.

"Ivy?" she says.

Her flashlight shines, fading the glowing words.

"What happened?" she asks, kneeling at my side. She pulls something from the wall, by the heating duct. An envelope with the number 13 inked onto it. She tears the envelope open, revealing a tarnished key ring with two keys attached.

I don't speak. I don't have words. I just crumple into her arms and wait for the music to stop.

THE MUSIC HAS FINALLY STOPPED. IVY'S FACE HAS
lost all color.

"Shayla's here," she whispers.

"How do you know for sure?"

"I heard her. She spoke to me."

"Or it seemed like she spoke to you," I say, ever the bearer of
reasonable doubt. "What if it just *sounded* like her voice…like if it
was an actor or something, and the voice had been prerecorded?"

"You just don't get it, do you? I heard Garth's voice too."

I bite my tongue and look down at the key ring in my hand. There are two keys attached, one bigger than the other. "Any guesses as to what these might go to?" I ask, dropping them into her palm.

"Maybe room thirteen," Ivy guesses. "Maybe that's where the others are being kept."

I bite my tongue harder and peer around the room. Without the candlelight, or aiming my flashlight at the walls, I can see pictures and writing everywhere—done with glow-in-the-dark paint. The words WHY?, I CAN'T, and I HATE IT are splattered by the door.

"We need to go downstairs," Ivy insists.

"Okay," I say, getting up, checking my watch. Two and a half hours left.

"How did you get the door to open?"

I pull a hairpin from my pocket. It's been bent into a lightning bolt. "In the words of Sebastian Slayer from *Forest of Fright:* 'Easy as squeezy. I love bein' cheesy.' A little trick I learned in acting camp to sneak into the green room after hours."

"I think that's the clue," she says, nodding to the heating vent, not even listening.

I shine my flashlight over it, unable to see a thing. "Am I missing something?"

She points my flashlight away so I can see 36 L written across the vent in the alien-green paint.

"Okay, no doubts about it," I say. "This is definitely part of a combination code for a lock or safe: twenty-eight R, thirty-six L . . . but we still need one more number. I'm telling you, somewhere in this creepy-ass place, there's a padlock with our names all over it."

Ivy takes her notepad from her bag and adds the new clue to her list, as well as the date May 9.

"What's that for?" I ask.

"The day of Ricky's death. April showers bring May flowers. . . ."

"Oh, right, how silly of me." I roll my eyes, completely oblivious.

"We need to go down to the basement," she says, ignoring my sarcasm, refusing to explain. "We need to—" She stops short, touching her earphones.

"What's he saying *now*?" I scoot back down to listen.

"I haven't even told you how Ricky died yet, have I, Princess?" he says. "Let me assure you that he made quite a statement. Awkward, introverted, did-all-his-work/never-sneezed-too-loud-or-laughed-too-hard/ate-every-last-morsel-on-his-plate Ricky chose center stage for his death. On the night of his suicide, he went down to the locker room and took a hot shower. If you haven't already seen signs for the locker room, it's two floors beneath you."

"Downstairs," Ivy says, her eyes wide with hope, no doubt imagining finding Shayla and the others. "Are *you* thinking what I'm thinking?"

"That I'm going to need serious therapy after today?"

"He seems to know a little too much about Ricky's death... since he was a student here *after* Ricky, I mean. He wasn't even around for the suicide."

"Are you kidding? Rumors that potent stay alive for years. For instance, there was this one girl who'd attended the same arts camp as me. Rumor had it that after rehearsals for the *Wizard of Oz*, she skipped down the yellow brick road with both the Tin Man *and* the Scarecrow... if you know what I mean."

"Not really." Ivy makes a confused face.

"The point is that even though her attendance at the camp was years before my time, the story was still legendary."

"Rumors in such detail, though?"

"He could just be elaborating."

"Or he could be Ricky himself."

"Except Ricky's supposed deadness puts a wrench in that theory, wouldn't you say?"

"Maybe it was only an attempted suicide."

"And maybe we should get going. Ticktock, ticktock," I say, reminding her. Our flashlights in hand, we scurry out of the room.

From the Journal of E.W.

Grade 7, August Preparatory School

SPRING 1972

I haven't written in a while. I've been too busy doing research on Ricky Slater. There are so many rumors about him—about what he did on the night he killed himself, and how he did it, and what he had with him. Kids say that Ricky was really weird and that he said strange stuff—like if they were talking about a cute girl, Ricky would try to fit in by saying how much he loved boobs. And he talked about the characters in books like they were real people, mumbling about their problems, and acting all concerned about the choices they were making.

Some kid whose mother works in the library said that the teachers didn't like him either, that his mother used to come to school and flirt with the old headmaster, spending hours in his office—even though they were both married.

Ricky's mother killed herself too, less than a year before his own death. Does suicide run in families? Word has it that after her suicide, Ricky got weirder, even giving the teachers the creeps. Kids say he stared too hard, lingered too long, and grinned at inappropriate times.

I saw a movie about ghosts the other day—about how this one ghost was haunting a girl because he wanted her to find a special coin he'd hidden while he was alive. After she found it, the ghost went away. If I do what Ricky wants, will he go away too?

Did Johnny leave Mother alone after she burned down the house? Part of me hopes that he didn't—that he'll haunt her until she dies. Another part wonders if maybe Mother was never being haunted at all. Maybe the ghost of Johnny was just an excuse to torture me.

IVY

WE MOVE THROUGH AN EXIT DOOR AT THE END OF
the hall. There are tiny spotlights positioned in the corners of the
ceiling, highlighting the stairwell.

Music starts playing. A peppy piano tune. A wiry male voice.
*"Wanna play dress-up, little girl, little girl? It's time for your makeup,
little girl, little girl. Blanched-white skin, like the dead. Lie still in a
satin bed. Dark-red lips, be still your breath. Little girl, little girl."*

"Where's it coming from?" Taylor asks.

It sounds as if it's far away—in another part of the building. Meanwhile, photos of me—from age twelve until just last

week—hang on the walls. Dozens of photos that show me walking home from school, getting on a bus, playing tennis off a wall, reading on my front porch.

"Holy hell!" Taylor shouts out, shining her flashlight on my eighth-grade graduation photo—with my full-on braces, bright orange hair (an attempt to transform my chestnut tresses into blond ones), and wire-rimmed eyeglasses.

"It's like he's in love with you," Taylor says.

"Not in love, just..."

"Starstruck?" she asks, finishing my thought, pointing at a crudely drawn star outlining my MVP soccer photo, done in green crayon.

I nod, thinking how in some twisted sort of way—despite the obvious creep factor—seeing all of these photos feels somewhat cathartic, because it helps explain the constant sensation I felt of being watched. Dr. Donna believed it was pure paranoia and prescribed pretty little pills to blot out what I was feeling. But here's proof that I wasn't being paranoid.

A locker room sign at the bottom of the stairs points us straight ahead and to the left. We're right near the tunnel. I peer down the hallway—the same one we passed before going upstairs, the one with the visible pipes. There are no spotlights here, nor one single candle. The music sounds even farther away now. "Shayla!" I shout.

"Holy darkness, Batgirl," Taylor says, moving down the hall, several steps in front of me.

Something squeaks. Taylor lets out a yelp. I shine my flashlight along the floor, suspecting there must be mice.

But instead I find something else.

A shoe.

Someone's leg.

I angle my flashlight upward, able to find a pair of eyes. I let out a gasp.

"This way," Taylor calls. Her voice is coming from a good distance away, but I have no idea where she is; I can no longer see her flashlight beam.

A door creaks open at the end of the hall and then slams shut. My pulse races. My legs start to tremble. I angle my flashlight to see who the eyes belong to.

Danny Decker.

I recognize him from the amusement park, as well as from *Nightmare Elf II*. His brother Donnie stands beside him. Dressed in tuxedos, the ten-year-old twins have slick black hair, ghost-white faces, and dark, dilated eyes that stare straight back at me.

"Taylor!" I shout.

She doesn't answer. She must've gone into the locker room.

Danny and Donnie's noses are bleeding. The blood drools over their lips and down their chins. "I'm so glad you've come to join us." They smile—red teeth, bloody tongues. "We've been waiting for you all day." They move to stand in the center of the hallway, blocking my path.

Piano music starts to play—the tune to "Three Blind Mice." They sing in unison: *"One blind mouse, one blind mouse. See how she runs, see how she runs. She thinks she's so much smarter than he. But he has a better plan, you see. Keep finding his clues, and you will be, one dead mouse. One dead mouse."*

I grab my knife and start to move past them, slicing through their image, the blade cutting through the air.

I hurry down the hallway. There are two doors at the end, one on each side. A locker room sign hangs crooked above one of them; it's been scribbled in red crayon, just like the WELCOME TO THE DARK HOUSE sign from the Nightmare Elf movies.

I go inside. Dim spotlights hover over rows of metal lockers, as well as a long wooden bench.

"Taylor?" I shout.

A trickle of something rolls toward my feet. I squat down to see what it is. At the same moment, there's a banging sound—a series of loud, hard clamors that stop my breath.

I turn toward the sound, covering over my ears. The locker room doors clank open and shut, open and shut. Meanwhile, the trickle on the floor rolls between my feet. It's red, like blood.

I go to get up, using the bench for leverage. My legs are shaking.

My heart is pounding. I catch myself from toppling over, my hand smacking down on the floor—into the stream of red.

"Taylor," I shout again, trying to yell out over the clamoring. I shiver at the sight of my palm—at the deep red color and its slimy consistency.

Finally, the clamoring stops. The spotlight overhead blinks. There must be a loose connection. I wipe my palm on my pants and look over at the rows of lockers. One of them has a lock. I approach it slowly, suspecting it must be number thirteen. With trembling fingers, I fish the key ring from my pocket.

The number thirteen is scratched and faded, but still it's clear. I push one of the keys into the lock. It turns with a click. I open the door latch.

A picture frame sits on the top shelf. It looks vaguely familiar, but it takes my brain a beat to process what it is.

As well as who it's of.

And where it's from.

It had sat on my real father's bedside table for years, but I hadn't thought about it until now. The killer must've taken it on the night of the murder. When the police went through their room, taping it off as a crime scene, I hadn't noticed that the picture was missing.

I take it from the shelf. A picture of me sits in the middle. I'm six years old, wearing a pink tutu for Halloween. The word "Princess" is printed at the top in pink bubble letters.

"Anything look familiar, Princess?" His voice crawls over my skin. "Just a little souvenir from your childhood home, but I thought you might like it back."

I clasp my hand over my mouth to hold back a cry. I couldn't hate him more.

"I'm sure that Ricky's very pleased with you so far . . . setting the note where it should've been placed to begin with, and now walking in his shoes. Slippers, actually." He snickers. "Ricky had been wearing slippers on the night of his death."

Next to the framed photo, there's a pair of slippers inside the locker, as well as an orange, a set of pajamas, and a thick roll of roping. I touch the pajamas; the flannel is stiff. The pant legs are faded and frayed. The initials on the shirt tag read R.S. Is it possible that these were really his?

"Who knows what Ricky had been thinking that night," the voice says. "Why did he have an orange? What possessed him to take a shower? Was it some sort of symbolic gesture of rebirth? A washing away of his sins? Did he simply want his body to be clean when found? Or perhaps the warm rush of water made him feel safe? I must admit, the answer has plagued me for years. But perhaps you can figure things out. Go find his shower stall now—the one in the far corner, against the wall."

The sound of glass breaking gives me a jolt. It came from the other side of the locker room.

Someone laughs—a high-pitched cackle that ripples down my spine.

I slip the picture frame into my bag and move around the corner. Ricky's stall is unmistakable. A spotlight shines over a series of dark red words dripping down the ceramic tile: WHY?; I CAN'T; I HATE IT.

"Of course, I've taken the liberty of re-creating the way the shower had looked that night," the voice continues. "But if you get real close, you can still see the marker he used. There's a trace of it on the tile, despite how hard the cleaners scrubbed. Go ahead and have yourself a peek."

I step inside the shower and bring the flashlight close to the tiles. He's right. Some of the original letters are still visible. I run my fingers over them; they're faded cries for help.

"I used to shower in the corner too, whenever the stall was available," he continues. "I'd imagine Ricky standing there, the water rushing against his face, and wonder what he'd been thinking—why he'd chosen those particular words."

I can't help wondering the same. What couldn't Ricky do? What was the answer to why?

"Stand beneath the faucet, Princess. And turn on the water. Let the warmth pour over your skin."

The inside of my mouth tastes like lead. The sound of glass breaking again cuts into my core.

"Remember, failure to follow my instructions will result in never seeing your co-stars again. Is that clear?"

It's as if he can read my mind.

I turn the faucet on, bracing myself for a gush of water. But it doesn't come—not even when I twist the valve all the way.

I look up at the spout. It's bone dry, not a drop of water. He's playing with me. I should've known better. Why would an abandoned building have running water to begin with?

"You'll find a marker on the soap dish," he continues. "Use it to add your own thoughts. What would your last words be?"

I take the marker and press the tip against the shower tile. A series of words and questions floods my brain, but the one phrase that screams the loudest is the one that I write down: GO TO HELL.

The high-pitched giggle repeats. It sounds as if it's coming from around another corner. I head in that direction—into the bathroom area. The mirrors are broken. Glass lies in the sinks and on the floor.

All of the bathroom stalls are open, except for the fourth one; the door is partway closed. I take a step toward it, noticing blood dripping onto the floor.

"Hello?" I call.

A pair of feet appears—clunky boots, dark tights. The person steps down from the toilet seat.

A whining sound comes from the door hinge, and yet the door doesn't move; it remains half-closed.

Natalie comes out. There's a wide smile on her cut-up face and a piece of glass in her blood-soiled hand. Her image wavers slightly as she brings the glass up to her face and makes a sideways slit. Blood drips down her neck, over her clothes, and onto the floor. "You know that I don't like mirrors, right?" Her voice sounds exactly as I remember it.

She moves over to the mirror and pounds her fists against the glass, producing the familiar shattering sound. "Seven years of bad luck," she says, grabbing another piece of glass. She turns in my direction, staring out into space. "You've had seven years of bad luck too, haven't you?" There are two pieces of glass in her hands now. She rubs them together, as though sharpening knives; there's a slashing sound. Then she moves back into the bathroom stall and climbs up on the toilet seat.

I wait for the scene to repeat—for her to come back out, so that I can go in. Once she does, I open the stall door wide. There are words above the toilet, written in bloodred lettering with someone's finger; I can see the fingerprint marks: RICKY WAS HERE BUT NOW HE'S DEAD, NOBODY EVER LISTENED TO A WORD HE SAID.

I search the stall: under the seat and in the toilet paper dispenser. I even remove the lid of the tank, knowing there must be a clue somewhere.

The sound of glass shattering startles me.

"Seven years of bad luck," Natalie repeats. "You've had seven years of bad luck too, haven't you?" Her voice is followed by the slish-slash sound as she rubs the blades of glass together.

She comes back into the stall. And climbs onto the seat. Frantic, I reach through her image—right into her gut—to pull up on the seat. She blinks her eyes; they're exactly as I remember them: light blue, dark makeup, a mole on her lower lid.

When she gets up again, I can see something sitting at the bottom of the toilet bowl. I reach in to grab it, but it jumps from my hands, moves deeper into the hole.

I pull up on my sleeve and reach in farther, my fingers grazing a box—plastic, the size of a cell phone. I pull it out and open it up. There's a slip of paper inside. I turn it over, my fingers trembling. It says 41R.

Forty-one Right?

The giggling starts up again. It's louder now. A piercing shrill. It sounds so familiar.

Music starts to blare—a guitar, drums, cymbals. I recognize the tune: "Wipe Out" by the Surfaris.

My heart quickens to the beat. I move out of the stall, passing right through Natalie, racing to get away.

TAYLOR

THIS CLEARLY ISN'T THE LOCKER ROOM. A LIGHTBULB fixture with an extension cord attached hangs down from a ceiling with exposed beams. It's like I've just walked onto the set of *Night Terrors III*—in the scene where high school junior Reva Foster plays hide-and-seek in an old, abandoned paper factory and ends up getting sliced and diced by a supersize paper shredder.

There are boxes of books everywhere, and random school supplies: a chalkboard, a photocopy machine, one of those rolling skeletons from bio class, and a human brain encapsulated in some jellylike substance and kept in a glass tank.

The room is long and narrow. I walk a little farther, spotting a lit candle on the floor. It highlights the word RICKY, written in big black capitals on the cracked cement, and crossed out with a giant X.

The candle sits in the center of a bunch of other items—a ceramic statue of the Virgin Mary, a string of rosary beads, a chalice, and a big chunky crystal.

I squat down in front of the candle, and a tendril of smoke floats up my nose. It smells like beeswax.

There's also a deck of index cards held together with a rubber band. The cards have yellowed with age. The corners are torn. The ink is smudged. I remove the band to take a closer look. It's hard to tell what they are. Poems? Chants? Prayers? I start to read one of them, but then the lightbulb blinks. There must be a loose connection. I stand, just as there's a knock on the door.

"Ivy?"

The knocking shifts to the back of the storage room. I look in that direction. There's writing on the chalkboard. The letters Y and O. It wasn't there before. The letter U is forming now, like phantom writing.

I scan the room, trying to find an explanation, in lieu of pissing my pants. Meanwhile, the phantom writing continues. I watch the words form, imagining myself on the set of a movie. *This is only for entertainment's sake*, I tell myself. *My role is to act scared.*

259

I blink hard, and then look back up at the board. It now reads YOU WILL . . .

. . . *be sorry you ever came here?* (Too late, I already am.)

. . . *wake up and discover this was just a nightmare?* (Could my subconscious be that cruel?)

. . . *piss your pants?* (Totally possible, though I'm dehydrated and starving to death.)

The light flickers again. I look up. The bulb seems brighter than before, blinding me, making me feel off balance. I glance away and try to refocus on the board. The message becomes clear: YOU WILL NEVER GET OUT.

My stomach sinks. My skin starts to sweat. The writing continues. The letters *L* and *O*.

I take a deep breath, spotting something move out of the corner of my eye. A shadow. A flash of light.

The bulb flickers again.

I look back at the chalkboard. Beneath the message are the words LOVE, RICKY.

I close my eyes a moment, channeling Neve Campbell's Sidney Prescott from *Scream*, in the scene where Sidney's on the phone with the killer, acting all ballsy, only to discover that he's actually inside the house, hiding in the closet, ready to pounce.

"Is someone there?" I ask, just as the light goes out altogether.

I squat back down, searching the floor for my flashlight. I put it down when I was checking out the index cards.

There's a bulb flashing sound. And a big burst of light. Someone's here, taking pictures.

"Who's there?" I shout, shielding my eyes from the blow of light.

Flash.

Flash.

Flash.

I creep forward, on my hands and knees, toward the door. I reach upward, searching for the knob, pounding my fists against the door panel. "Ivy!" I shout.

Footsteps move in my direction. There's a deep-throated giggle.

Flash.

Flash.

My back up against the door, I face the room, trying to mentally prepare myself for what comes next.

"Who's there?" I call again, my heart racing. There's a spray of colors in front of my eyes.

A moment later, I fall backward. The door's whipped open, and I tumble onto my back, into the hallway.

Ivy's there. She must've heard me.

"Someone's in there," I tell her, able to hear the fear in my voice.

Ivy points her flashlight inside. I move to stand behind her, making sure the door doesn't close. Her flashlight shines over the skeleton, the brain, the religious stuff.

The chalkboard is clear now—no writing. The candle's been extinguished. And I don't see a single soul.

"Your flashlight," she says, nodding to it, on the floor by the brain tank.

I hurry to snatch it up and then I shut the door behind us.

IVY

"WHAT THE HELL WERE YOU DOING IN THERE?" I ASK.

"Let's go," Taylor says, speeding past me down the hallway.

I hurry to keep pace beside her. "What happened?" I insist.

She doesn't answer. She just keeps on moving—past where I saw the Decker twins and back through the tunnel. Eventually, we're spit out into the hallway we first entered—the one with the snapshots of Frankie and Shayla.

"Taylor!" I shout, talking to her back.

Finally, she turns to face me.

"Are you going to tell me what happened?" I ask her. "And what you were even doing in that room?"

"Clearly not my nails." She angles her flashlight over her chipped green polish. "Look, I'd really rather forget the last twenty or so mortifying minutes of my life, but suffice it to say that I want to go—like now. Are you with me? This is an old building. There's got to be a way—a crack, a hole, a balcony window that I can jump out."

"You know I can't."

She grinds her teeth. Her eyes roll up toward the ceiling. And she balls up her fists.

"I'm sorry," I tell her, but only for disappointing her, not for wanting to stay. "But I need to see this through."

"This is insane. You know that, right?"

I shrug. My heart sinks. "My whole life has been insane. But yours hasn't. That's the difference. I understand if you want to go."

"Okay, fine," she says, after a five-second pause. She takes a deep breath and looks directly at me again. Her eyes are watery. Her upper lip trembles. "I'll stay. But when this is all done, you owe me big time. I see a major spa day in my future, and not just a measly mani-pedi either. I'm talking facial, brow wax, salt scrub, the works." There's a smile on her face, and yet tears streak down her cheeks.

"Are you sure?" I ask her.

"About the spa day? Yes. About enduring another minute of this funked-up-crazy shit? Hell no. But I can't jump ship—not without you, that is."

I give her a hug. She quivers in my embrace. It feels weird being the brave one—empowering and unsettling at once.

Instead of going back to the lobby, we move through the door at the end of the hall.

"Where are we going?" Taylor asks.

I lead her down the stairwell, headed for the basement.

There's a steel door at the bottom of the stairs. I shine my flashlight over it, noticing a metal box above the knob with a blinking red light.

"What's that?" she asks.

There's a keypad on the box. I try the knob; unsurprisingly, it doesn't turn. "We need to enter a code."

"One that we're bound to get on one of these crazy-ass challenges. I really think we need to get all of our ducks in a row first."

"Excuse me?" She sounds like a grandma. "You hardly strike me as a planner."

"You're right." Taylor sighs. "I'm a fly-by-the-seat-of-my-pants kind of girl, but still that doesn't change my mind."

Except we're running out of time. I focus back down at the keypad and type in the words *Nightmare Elf*. A red *X* appears.

Too easy. The code word needs to be something more clever.

I try Dark House, Parker Bradley, Ivy Jensen, my old name (April Leiken), my parents' names (Sarah and Matthew Leiken). I go to type in Ricky Slater, but the keypad doesn't work. The buttons no longer push.

I'm cut off.

My chest tightens.

I slam my fist against the door, hoping to get another shot— that I'm only allowed a certain number of tries, within a certain amount of time, before the keypad locks up.

"I hate to say *I told you so*, but..." Taylor chides.

I rest my forehead against the door. "They're in there," I whisper. "Shayla's in there. I heard her. Natalie called me."

"On the phone? I thought your cell was dead."

"Before, I mean. In the parking lot at the police station." I don't have time to explain. I need to crack this code. I take out my notebook and scribble down the new clue. "Forty-one R," I say aloud.

"It obviously supports the locker combination theory."

"How are we doing for time?"

"An hour and a half left."

"We need to get to the theater," I tell her.

"How do you know?"

"Because after Ricky took his shower, that's where he went. Center stage."

"Upstairs," Taylor says. "I saw a sign for the auditorium."

266

We race back upstairs, down the hall, and through the lobby. As we pass by the library, I'm able to hear the familiar music—the piano playing and Denise Kilborn's voice.

"That way." Taylor shines her flashlight over a double set of doors. A sign for the theater/auditorium hangs over them.

We step inside. It's dark, but a light clicks on, illuminating the center stage. A noose hangs from the ceiling, wavering back and forth, as if someone just touched it.

"It's show time, Princess," his voice whispers into my ear. "Go have yourself a seat. I've reserved the front row just for you."

Taylor takes my hand and gives it a squeeze. Slowly, we walk down the aisle, toward the stage. I keep my eyes focused on the noose, imagining a body hanging from it: feet dangling, eyes open, limbs pooled with blood.

"There," Taylor says, bringing me back to earth, pointing to the front row. A bouquet of dead roses rests on one of the seats.

I move closer, noticing two cardboard buckets tucked beneath the seats, filled with movie snacks—popcorn, soda, Sno-Caps, Jujyfruits.

"I wonder if he can hear the growling of my gut." Taylor plops down in a seat and starts digging into her bucket o' crap, like it's a Saturday afternoon and we're here to see a movie.

"Do you like your view of the stage, Princess?" the voice asks. "Ricky hung himself during his sophomore year. I'd see his body

267

throughout my school day—in the shower, out the window, in the corner of every classroom. Dangling, swaying, eyes open, mouth arched wide. You know a thing or two about being haunted, don't you, Princess?" There's amusement in his voice.

A screen drops down in front of the noose. The lights go out. My skin starts to itch.

Parker and I appear on the screen. We're lying in bed, facing one another—me, beneath the covers; him, on top of them.

"Holy shit," Taylor mutters.

A lump forms in my throat.

"I'm assuming that's at the Dark House," Taylor says.

"It is." I nod.

She doesn't say anything. Meanwhile, I can't help feeling everything: angst, frustration, sadness, regret.

On the screen, Parker swipes a lock of hair from in front of my eyes. The camera angles on his face, highlighting the upturn of his lips. *"You're pretty cool, you know that?"*

The sound of his voice sends a shockwave through my body.

"You're only saying that because you feel sorry for me," I tell him.

He makes a confused face. *"What's to feel sorry for?"*

"You're kidding, right?" I smile and roll my eyes. My hair's draped over the pillow, and there's an unfamiliar glow on my face. I look so happy, despite where I am.

"I'm not kidding," he says. *"So take a compliment, okay?"*

From the Journal of E.W.

Grade 7, August Preparatory School

SPRING 1972

The headmaster pulled me into his office yesterday and said that teachers have told him I'm not doing well in classes and that everybody's worried. He called my grandparents, but they told him I was just fine if not a little homesick. I know this because Gramps called me right after and said that if I don't start shaping up, he'd lock me up in the funny house with my mother.

Kids have stopped sitting with me at lunch. They don't want me to be on their teams at recess or to sit with me in the library. But I don't really care. I don't need any of them. I have movies to keep me company. They show one every Saturday night in the rec room. Even if I don't like the movie pick, I'm happy just sitting there in the dark, where nobody else can see me, guessing at the director's choices for casting and camera angles. I analyze the story, asking myself questions about motivation and plot. Sometimes I even take notes.

Jarrod told me that everyone's comparing me to Ricky, saying I'm weird, different, spooky, strange. Jarrod asked why my eyes are always so red, why I don't dress neatly, and why I've been mumbling to myself.

"Who are you always talking to?" he asked.

"Nobody," I told him.

"Well, tell Nobody to shut up." He laughed.

I had to hold myself back from smashing him in the face. And I did, because I wanted to know: "Hey, do you still hear that knocking on the walls of your room?"

It took him a second to remember what he'd told me, and when he did, a grin appeared on his face. "I was just playing with you, man. Nothing like that ever happened for real."

"Then why did you lie?"

"Why not?" He laughed again. "To keep the legend going. It makes this place a lot less boring."

I hated him for that. I hate everyone here now. And I hate Ricky the most. I'm not like him at all. I'm smarter and more in control—maybe even a little like Mother. Once I do what Ricky says and find his suicide note, he's in for a big surprise.

NATALIE

"GET UP," THE ELF TELLS ME.

I do as he says, but not too quick—slow, slow, slow—imagining that my limbs are filled with lead.

"You need to appear weak," Harris says.

The Elf reaches through the bars. There's a cup in his hand. The tips of his glove are dirty. From chimney soot? Or filling stockings with coal? Is it Christmas already?

"Drink this," he tells me.

I take the cup, imagining eggnog.

"Don't," Harris says.

I nod—to Harris—holding the cup at my lips, allowing only my teeth to touch the liquid. I tilt my head back just enough for this to look real. There's a sweet taste: lemon and honey. My tongue really wants it. My throat croaks to get it. It's so hard not to gulp it down.

When the Elf turns his back to pour a second cup, I dump the liquid inside my coat. I'll be on Santa's naughty list for sure.

I smack my lips, make a soft "yum" sound, and picture a snowy day, wanting to pull so bad. In my mind, I grab a clump of hairs behind my ear, where it's been growing real good, and give a nice yank.

I twitch. My pulse races. My insides feel jumpy.

"*Go sit down,*" Harris says.

"Okay."

"Okay?" The Elf turns back to me. His eyes find mine from behind his mask. He presses his face against the bars of the cell. "I'm just a turn of the key away."

His singsongy voice sends chills down my spine, but I pretend not to be affected. I'm too weak and tired to be affected. I imagine warm teabags on my eyelids, while trying to hold my eyes open.

I move to the back of the cell and melt down against ground, as if there's no other logical choice—as if I'll collapse if I don't get down fast.

"*Very nice,*" Harris compliments me.

I love making him happy.

TAYLOR

I REACH THE BACK OF THE AUDITORIUM, DESPITE Ivy's pleas for me to stop and turn around. As I suspected, there's a stairwell that leads upstairs to the balcony. It's tucked in the corner, behind an American flag.

I proceed up the steps, using my flashlight to guide the way. I didn't want to say anything to Ivy, but I could've sworn I saw some curtains or drapes flapping up there, as though in the breeze. If that's the case, then there must be an open window.

I reach the top step. It's dark, but there are candles sprinkled about the space, making my stomach churn. This is a setup.

I haven't uncovered the secret cave that houses the precious jewel.

Still, I point my flashlight toward the billowing drapes—a good fifteen feet away. They hang from a giant window, with no bars and no boards. It appears wide open.

A trick? A trap?

I peer over the balcony, searching for Ivy, but she's no longer standing at the front of the theater. She must've moved backstage.

I point my flashlight toward the window again, able to see the darkening sky. It's gray out. It must be approaching dusk.

Slowly I begin toward the window, aiming my flashlight all around—in all corners, along the walls, at the ceiling, and even behind me—but I don't see anything suspect, aside from the candles and the window itself.

Is it possible that the candles are part of a scene he's staging for later? And that he left the window open simply to get some fresh air? What are the odds that he'd guess I'd see the curtains flapping and venture my way up here?

Just a few feet from the window now, the cool, crisp air blows against my cheeks. I breathe it in, able to smell the promise of snow, wondering how far up I am.

I take another step, just as my body falls forward. I drop downward. My chin smacks down against a ledge. My teeth clank together. I tumble onto my side.

A trick floor.

I'm in a hole.

Three feet down.

My flashlight still gripped in my hand, I shine it all around. There's a blue tarp lining the hole. It makes a crunch sound as I move to sit up, trying to get my bearings.

Footsteps move in my direction. I can hear the sound of the floor creaking. I scoot back against the wall, able to see someone's shoes; the tips inch out over the hole.

He's holding a lantern in his bright green glove. It dangles right above me. I shield my eyes from the light.

"Hello, Ms. Monroe. Thanks so much for *dropping by*." The sound of his voice makes me wince. "Some things never change, do they?"

"Change?" I ask; the word comes out shaky.

He peeks down into the hole. He isn't wearing a mask. A bad sign—the *worst* sign. I'm going to be sick. The killer only shows his face if he knows the victim will die.

"You were going to escape, weren't you? By sneaking out the window? Thinking only of yourself again, leaving Ivy on her own?"

"No," I say, shaking my head. "I was only going to look—to check the window out, to see how far down it was. I wouldn't leave without Ivy."

"Tell that to poor Natalie and the other Dark House Dreamers."

"Please," I beg. "I'll do whatever you want. You're the director," I say, as if he needs a reminder. "You can make it look like I died, but then it could be a trick. You could have me come back for the next movie—to round out the trilogy. I could be the perfect plot twist."

He stares at me—a wrinkled face, a scar down his cheek, the tiniest eyes I've ever seen. There's a curious smile across his lips, as if he might actually be considering the idea.

"I'm a scream queen," I continue to beg. "I was made for this stuff, trained by the very best. How about if I go back downstairs—back to Ivy? I'll tell her anything you want. She trusts me. Use that, use *me*."

His curious smile grows bigger. "That's a very generous offer, but no one likes a traitor, especially not in horror movies. They're often the first to die. Now be a good girl and shut off your flashlight."

"Please," I beg.

"Now, Ms. Monroe."

I do as he says and click it off. At the same moment, I see the glimmer of a blade.

"No!" I shout.

"I'm very sorry, Ms. Monroe, but your role has been cut."

The lantern goes out. My world turns dark. The last sounds I hear are the crinkling of the tarp and the screaming of a voice.

Ivy

THE BUZZER STOPS. IT'S MORGUE SILENT. I STAND and shine my flashlight around the theater, looking for Taylor.

A thwack sound cuts through the silence: The doors at the back of the auditorium slam shut.

"Ivy?" Parker's voice.

I turn to look, my pulse racing. There's a tunneling sensation inside my heart.

Parker's there, on the screen. At first I assume it's more footage from the Dark House weekend. But then I see what it really is:

Parker sitting in a dark room, mostly hidden in shadows, much like the video of Natalie.

I can tell that it's him from his silhouette—his wavy hair, his broad chest, his long legs, and the muscles in his forearms. I recognize his sneakers too—black cross-trainers with bright green stripes.

"I've been told that you're coming here," he says. "I hope that isn't true. You've been through enough." He leans forward slightly, and I'm able to see his strong jawline and a flash of his blond hair. "There's a lot I want to tell you, but so much that I can't say." He rests his hand on his knee. There's something wrapped around his wrist. A rope? A chain? He moves his leg and the image becomes clear.

A narrow, cylindrical shape.

The bottle pendant charm. My aromatherapy necklace. It dangles against his kneecap, sending chills all over my skin.

"Please be careful, Ivy. Please know that nothing's worth your safety. I have a—"

His voice is cut short, cut off.

My hand trembles over my mouth. What was he trying to say? What did he want to tell me?

Is it a coincidence that his words were cut off in the very same spot as my mom's? Those were her very last words before the killer took her life. "*I have a . . .*"

The screen fades to pale gray. There's the shadow of someone on a swing now: a billowy dress, clunky boots, a mass of hair.

"Natalie?" I shout.

I move closer to the stage, trying to see if the person swinging is behind the screen. But there's only about a six-inch gap between the floor of the stage and the bottom of the screen. I don't see feet, nor do I see the shadow of anything moving behind the screen.

The silhouette continues to swing, back and forth. Whoever it is turns her head; a massive bubble blows out her mouth.

A moment later, the bubble pops, and I hear the snapping-sucking of bubble splat as she takes the gum back into her mouth. The noises sound live—like they're happening in real time and not part of any film.

"Who's there?" I ask.

"I'm not allowed to tell you," a voice says from behind the screen.

"Natalie?" I repeat; my heart throbs. It sounds just like her voice—same tone, same crackling quality.

"I can't talk right now." She jumps off the swing. The motion of the shadow matches the thump sound.

I rush up the stairs that lead to the stage. There's no one behind the screen. There's no swing either.

Only the noose is there. It dangles under a spotlight. "Natalie?"

I call, even though it probably wasn't her; it was probably just a trick. My voice cracks the silence, causes my blood to stir.

I grab my knife and move closer to the stage curtain. There's a tiny hallway that leads backstage. A shuffling noise comes from that direction. I follow the sound, unable to stop shaking. The knife tremors in my grip.

Just then, a blast of air punches me—blows against the side of my face—and I let out a wail. It came from a wall vent.

"Back here." Natalie's voice.

I move in deeper, feeling my body turn to ice.

A body hangs down from the ceiling. Ricky Slater's. The image of his naked body wavers back and forth. His skin is gray. His eyes are rolled upward. The veins in his feet are swollen.

I stand, frozen, noticing a trickle of blood running from his nose, onto the towel beneath him. More blood trickles from his ear and down his neck.

I start to back away, just as his head tilts forward and his eyes refocus.

He looks right at me. "I'll haunt you for life," he whispers.

I take a few more steps back, bumping into something from behind. Six feet tall, freckled face, short blond hair, and dressed in a schoolboy uniform; a mannequin of Ricky stares straight ahead.

My face only inches from his chest, I second-guess myself that it isn't real. But I can't detect a breath. And his eyes have yet to blink. I reach out to touch the face, just as his arm flies up.

Like a reflex, I jam my knife into his gut. The arm continues to move, bending at the elbow.

I tear open his shirt, where the knife made an incision. The body's plastic. There are screws and bolts.

"Ivy!" Natalie's crying now; I can hear it in her voice.

I pull the knife free and move farther behind the stage. There are more dolls here, against a wall—at least a dozen of them. Mannequins with made-up faces, wearing elaborate costumes. A king and queen, a pauper, a knight, a man with a horse's head, a couple of prep school girls, a swamp creature with webbed feet.

"I'll haunt you for life," Ricky repeats.

His voice is followed by whispering. I can't tell where it's coming from. By the image of Ricky hanging? Behind the mannequins somewhere? I turn round and round, keeping a firm grip on my knife, trying to find the source.

And that's when I see him.

Out of the corner of my eye.

The Nightmare Elf.

Blood rushes from my head, makes everything feel dizzy, desperate, dark, vacant. Was that a grin? Did he mouth the word "Princess"?

I try to breathe through the stifling sensation, but the air gets caught in my lungs. A gasp escapes from my throat.

I blink hard, wondering if I'm seeing things, unable to even find him now. He was behind the queen, wasn't he? There was an ax in his hand, wasn't there? I shine my flashlight over the mannequins' plastic faces. Their eyes gape open, as if staring out into space. Their mouths are parted as if they have something to say.

I strain my eyes, wondering if he might be tucked behind the queen's dress. I aim my flashlight at the floor, trying to spot his boots, unable to find anything.

The whispering continues again, as does Natalie's crying. I stumble forward, beyond the mannequins. There's a narrow hallway to the right. It's lined on both sides with racks of costumes. I move slowly, angling my flashlight all around. The whispers get louder. My pulse is racing faster. The wings of a ladybug costume stick out into the aisle. I go to push them in, startled by what I see.

A red-haired boy, crouched on the floor, hiding in the costumes, holding a statue of the Virgin Mary. His body is transparent; he's almost hard to see. "Is it safe to come out yet?" he asks me.

I move past the boy, where the whispering seems more audible. There's a heat duct by the floor. I scoot down and press my ear up against it.

"You should read this, not that," a male voice whispers. "You should look up, not down. You should study harder, not longer.

You should speak loudly and clearly. You should think twice before speaking at all. My life is an endless black tunnel of should."

It's part of Ricky's suicide note.

I listen until the end, wondering if I'll hear anything else. But instead the whispering continues. The note's read from the beginning: "I'm sorry for what I've done, but I couldn't bear listening to the voices anymore. They creep up on me in the middle of the night and sneak beneath my bedcovers to whisper into my ear...."

I get up. My legs wobble.

A scream sounds, erupting in the space, rattling my nerves, causing the stage to vibrate. My mind tells me to hurry, but my body is stuck. Motionless. Color fades from in front of my eyes; my whole world darkens and swirls.

Another scream. Taylor's voice. I'm screaming too, but no sound comes out. Still, I try to remind myself: *I'm stronger than my fears. Bigger than this moment. What I need to accomplish is more important than being scared.*

I repeat this mantra inside my head until I'm finally able to move my feet. The static fades from in front of my eyes. I take a few steps, so focused on the stage curtain that I bump into the mannequin of Ricky again. It makes a shifting noise. I make a gagging sound.

Did someone just tug my hair?

"I'll haunt you for life," a voice plays again.

Back out on the stage, I don't see Taylor. I look upward, just as the overhead spotlights turn on.

Whoosh.

Whoosh.

Click.

The lights shine over the stage, the seats, the center and side aisles. The doors at the back of the theater are open again. The balcony, where Taylor was headed, is lit up as well. I can see a video projector and some other technical equipment, but she's nowhere in sight.

"Taylor," I shout, tears sliding down my face.

Ricky's whispering starts up again. It's louder now, coming from the speakers as well as from my headset. There are other voices too, all of them overlapping, making it hard to decipher whose voice goes with what's being said:

"There's a lot I want to tell you, but so much that I can't say."

"It looked like I died, didn't it? Like a giant piece of pointed glass fell on top of my head. But I was able to step back, thanks to Harris's warning. He has a warning for you too."

"What no one seems to realize is that I hate myself even more than they do, and that the voices in my head are the loudest ones of all."

"Are you there?" Shayla's voice. *"I'm downstairs."*

Holding the knife in one hand and the flashlight in the other, my first instinct is to move the headset away and cover my ears.

But instead I stand at center stage. The noose is still there. There's something attached to it. An envelope dangles from the loop of the rope. Was it there before? Is it possible I'm just noticing it? I take the envelope. The loop is at eye level. I picture it around my neck, imagine it squeezing my throat. I turn the envelope over. Scribbled across the front is #4B. I tear it open. There's a tiny candle inside, as well as a slip of paper. I turn the paper over to read the words, printed in black block letters: IT'S TIME TO PAY YOUR RESPECTS.

"What is that supposed to mean?" I shout. But my voice goes unheard, drowned out by all the others.

IVY

"TAYLOR!" I SHOUT, MOVING OFF THE STAGE. I scurry down the center aisle, shining my flashlight all around, looking for some sign of her.

Back out in the hallway, I call her name a dozen more times. My voice echoes off the ceilings and walls, producing little more than a throat that feels raw and bleeding.

I move toward the lobby area, thinking of it as our meet-up spot. On the way there, I check the numbers on all the doors, searching for #4B, like it said on the envelope, wondering if it might be a room number.

Room number 4 is a tiny space; it was probably once an office. But there's no adjoining room connected to it.

"Taylor?" I call, peering around the lobby.

She isn't here.

There's no sound.

Anxiety bubbles up in my gut. Tears streak down my face. I fold to the floor, feeling like I'm going to be sick.

"I hate you!" I scream at the top of my lungs, wishing he'd take me instead. I gaze upward at the cross on the wall, remembering church on Sundays with my birth parents. They'd had so much faith, put so much stock in God's word. We used to give thanks before our meals, and pray before bed too. Mom always said that everything happens for a reason—that even when something seems difficult or inexplicable, it's part of God's plan.

Was their death part of His plan as well? Was losing the others? Or coming here?

"Take me!" I cry out, over and over again, until my throat burns raw. But nothing happens and still I remain.

Alone.

Empty.

Guilty.

Nauseated.

I look up at the cross again, picturing Taylor in my mind. "Please," I whisper, reminding myself how smart and resourceful she is, how she was the one who made it out of the Dark House, after all—the one who figured out, after barely an hour, that it wasn't a safe place to be. *Please, be okay*, I repeat inside my head, hoping that someone is listening, feeling entirely responsible.

If it weren't for the killer's obsession with me, the others would all be safe.

If it weren't for my obsession with the case, Taylor would never have come here.

I tuck myself into a ball, barely able to move, unsure if I can breathe. After several moments, I'm finally able to reach into my bag for my bottle of water.

My hand finds my container of pills first. I'm supposed to take the green one every day, as well as three of the peach, and the tiny yellow ones as needed. The white ones are for sleepless nights.

A whole rainbow of barbiturates.

It's been days since I've had even one.

I go to shake a green one onto my palm, but two of them come out instead, along with a peach and two yellows. I pop them into my mouth and chase them down with a swig of water, hoping to get a grip, desperate to numb this ache.

It doesn't take long before I start to feel the effects. My stomach's empty. I haven't slept. I picture the capsules dissolving inside my gut, the contents absorbed inside my veins. The chemicals warm me up like toast, filling all of my cold, dank spaces.

Is the knife still clenched in my hand? Or did I put it back in my bag? I go to check, but something distracts me.

Footsteps?

Music?

What was I checking for?

Am I supposed to blow out all of the candles? Switch off all the spotlights?

I'm so unbelievably tired. My eyelids feel heavy.

"Don't fall asleep," a female voice says.

Taylor? My eyes won't open.

"April, honey." Mom's fingers cradle my palm.

I feel sick. I'm going to yack. Did I eat Miko's stuffed waffles?

"You've been through a lot." Dr. Donna's voice. *"Post-traumatic stress disorder can do that; it can impair your ability to distinguish what's real from what isn't."*

"Do you want to be an actress?" Parker asks me.

"Apparently I'm not a very good one if you're onto me already," I say. *"Can you keep a secret? I hate horror. Like, I* really *hate it. I don't get what the appeal is . . . why someone would ever want to be scared."*

"Please, April. Get rid of it. Use your fingers; stick them down your throat." Mom rubs my back; a warm, comforting sensation.

"You're one of the chosen, here for the party. Stay for the rolling credits, why don't you?" Garth?

"Ready, Princess? It's time to pay your respects."

I picture my fingers inside my mouth, inching toward my throat. Is it really happening? Am I really doing it?

There's a rumble in my gut and an acidic taste in my mouth. My mind says sit up and yet I'm still lying on the ground. My head aches. My mouth fills; I spit onto the floor.

My stomach lurches again. More liquid spews out—again and again and again—until nothing is left except the reflex of purging and the sound of my retching.

My eyes are watery. My nose burns. No one else is here. But still I can still feel my mother's hand on my back, as though I'm suddenly not alone.

Ivy

I SIT UP AND GAZE AROUND. THE LOBBY APPEARS AS it did before—the lit candles, the evil-children-reading statue, the cross on the wall. There's a sickly sour smell in the air.

I start to get up, but my head feels woozy and my limbs are heavy. How much time remains on the clock?

I make sure that everything's still in my bag, and then I stumble out of the lobby, hating myself for taking those pills.

It's time to pay my respects. I remember having spotted the chapel from the courtyard; it was on the right side of the building.

It looked as if it'd been added on; the stone didn't match the rest of the building.

I proceed down the hallway, past the library and auditorium, still looking around for any sign of Taylor and the others. It's quiet again—there's only the crunching of my feet as I walk over broken floor tile and the beating of my heart; it reverberates inside my ears.

"Come on," a male voice says.

I shine my flashlight at the ceilings and walls, unable to tell where the voice came from—not from my headset or from any overhead speaker. Was it just in my head?

There's a narrow door at the end of the hall. I move toward it, wondering if the voice might've come from the other side of it.

"Better watch your back," the voice says.

"Frankie?" I ask. There's a ringing in my ears.

"Come on," he says again; his voice seems louder now, as if it's definitely coming from behind the door. Is he locked up? Or talking to someone else? Or maybe this is a trick. Or probably this is a trick.

I stop a couple feet from the door and grab the sides of my head. *"What do I do?"* a voice asks. It takes me a moment to realize that it's mine—my voice, my doubt.

But what if it really *is* him? What if something good will happen? What if I lose it right here, right now?

"You can't stop living," his voice says.

"Frankie?" I ask again, reaching out to touch the door handle, wanting so badly to believe it's him, and not another trick. And not my imagination.

The knob turns. The door opens. My heart sinks.

No Frankie.

No anyone.

There's another dark tunnel; it must join the two buildings. I hold my flashlight high. The walls are blank. The ceiling looks cracked. "Frankie?" I shout; the blare of my voice makes my head ache.

I begin toward the door at the end, but then I feel myself fall. My foot plummets through a hole. The floor collapses beneath my step. My knee lands hard against a jagged edge.

I shine my flashlight over the damage. My pants are ripped. Blood covers my knee. About two feet of flooring has caved in.

On my hands and one knee, I climb out of the hole to get onto a solid surface. At the same moment, the door slams shut behind me. I pull a scarf out of my bag—the wool one I used to hide the knife—along with a tiny bottle of tea tree oil. I douse the scarf, hoping the oil's antiseptic qualities will be good enough for now. Then I wind the scarf around my knee—tight—to stop the bleeding.

I begin down the tunnel again, cautious of each step. A crackling sound stops me.

A child's voice begins: *"Now I lay me down to rest. I pray my guardians will protect me best. But if I die at Ricky's will, I pray that I'll do worse than kill."*

I shine my flashlight behind me, above me, on the floors, at the walls. I'm still alone. There's no one else here. Breathe in, breathe out. It's just a scare tactic—an audio track piped through a speaker.

The prayer repeats over and over as I move toward the end of the tunnel. Once there, I open the door. The smell of burning candles and something else—sandalwood incense—hits me in the face, makes me feel nauseated.

I've found the chapel. It's tiny—ten rows of pews, maybe. The altar is piled with flowers. A podium stands in the middle.

I walk down the center aisle and take a seat in the first pew, noticing the arrangement of candles. A tall, thick candle stands in the center of what looks like hundreds of smaller ones.

I bow my head to play along, while thoughts and questions fog my mind. Was I dreaming about my mother in the lobby? Was it her hand I felt on my back? "April showers bring May flowers." Was that the purpose of that clue—to get me to turn the page in the calendar? To see that Ricky killed himself on May 9?

May 9. I picture the big black *X* over the date, feeling my body chill.

I get up, still playing by the rules, to approach the altar. I fish the candle from my pocket and light it from the flame of the large center candle.

At the same instant, I see it.

Stuck to the dripping wax, like a bright shining star.

A gold key.

I grab the candle. Hot wax drips onto my trembling fingers, searing the skin, making me wince. I dig my thumb into the wax, trying to pluck the key free. Finally it falls into my grip and I'm able to run for my life.

From the Journal of E.W.

Grade 7, August Preparatory School

SPRING 1972

I found Ricky's suicide note. He hid it in his favorite book. He wants me to share it, but that would mean letting him win, and I'll never let him win.

What Ricky doesn't seem to get is that I'm in control of my life. I decide how the scenes play out. Unlike Mother (if she was really being haunted by Johnny) I will never bow down to the enemy. To be a star means to face the demon and to slay him in the end.

So I'm keeping the note. I'm not going to show anyone. Ricky can rot away in Purgatory for all the misery he's caused me. I don't even care if he continues to haunt me. I'll just use it as inspiration for my movies. The movies I'm going to make one day.

IVY

I HURRY BACK THROUGH THE TUNNEL, HEADED FOR the other side of the building. In the lobby, I stop a moment to catch my breath, to take out my notebook, to make sure that I have everything.

I flip open to the page with the clues and read over the list—the padlock combination, the April showers riddle, the 4B number—suddenly realizing that I don't even know what 4B means.

A wave of panic storms my body. I touch my T-shirt bracelet, thinking about Parker. He's down there. I know he is. I have the code. I need to try.

Ticktock, ticktock. I recheck my pocket. The key ring (with the two keys) and the gold key are still there. This is still real. The air feels colder somehow.

I strap my bag across my body and move down the hallway. The photographs of Shayla, Garth, and Frankie are no longer here. I should've taken them earlier—should've stuffed them in my bag.

My heart pummels with each step toward the door at the end of the hall. I push through it and move down the staircase, wondering if the *B* in 4B might stand for basement.

At the foot of the stairs, I try the knob—just in case. It's still locked. The red light continues to blink. I type May 9 onto the keypad.

A red *X* appears.

I try again, picturing the desk calendar in my mind: 05-09-66.

A buzzer sounds. A green light flashes. The hairs at the back of my neck stand on end. I try the knob; it turns.

I open the door. A long corridor faces me. There are spotlights along a ceiling with exposed pipes and overhead ductwork. The lights shine over life-size cardboard cutouts.

The first one is of me, wearing the purple sundress from the Dark House weekend and holding the bottle pendant around my neck. My face is full of uncertainty—my brow furrowed, my lips pressed together.

Behind my cutout are those of Parker, Shayla, Frankie, Garth, and Natalie. Shayla's wearing the same tracksuit that she arrived to the Dark House in, with the cropped jacket that showed off her navel piercing. She's smiling—a wide, contagious grin, as if caught in a laugh.

Parker's cutout is just behind hers. His mouth is open in angst. His eyes are red with tears. He's standing in front of the exit gate, trapped inside the amusement park.

"Parker?" I shout, trying to be strong. "Taylor? Are you down here?"

I continue past the cutouts, noticing doors on both sides of the corridor; they're numbered with the letter *B*.

1 B.

3 B.

5 B.

4 B.

A weathered gray door. A combination lock holds it closed. The lights go out. I'm in the dark. I hear an evil giggle; it steels me in place.

"I'm so glad you decided to return to the Dark House, my Princess." The killer's voice, inside my ear.

I press my back against the wall, trying to breathe at a normal rate and feel stable on my feet.

"Well, I, for one, had no doubts," he says. "I know a shining star when I see one, and you certainly don't disappoint. We have so much in common, you and I. Though I was initially terrified by Ricky's hauntings, my own desire to win trumped my fear. You're terrified of me, and yet you're here, determined to win as well. Sometimes it's the things that scare us most that offer the greatest lessons. Don't ever lose sight of that, my Princess."

I scoot down to be at eye level with the lock. I angle my flashlight over the numbers. My hand is shaking. My mind is racing. I turn the dial to the right, to #28, but then my flashlight drops and rolls across the floor. I scurry to retrieve it by the foot of Natalie's cutout—her clunky black boot.

I pick the flashlight up; the beam catches her cardboard face: her cut-up lips, her eyes focused at the floor.

I try the lock again—28 to the right; 36 to the left; 41 to the right. It doesn't work, even when I pull, yank, and wrench the lock with all my might. I tumble back on the floor, landing smack on my butt. I get up and try again, slower this time.

My hand continues to tremble, but I'm able to get to 41 Right once more. I hold my breath and pull.

The lock opens and clatters to the floor. I pick it up, stuff it into my bag, and open the door. The hinges whine.

There's a large, open cellar area with crude cement walls. It's dark except for a dim light in the far corner. It shines over an antique-looking trunk. The rest of the space appears empty. The stench of mildew lingers in the air. Acid travels to the back of my throat.

I cross the room to open the trunk. The lid lifts up with an unsettling creak.

My bottle pendant lies on top, making me feel sick. Why doesn't Parker still have it? What does this mean?

Sitting beside the necklace is Frankie's infinity bracelet—the one that his mother gave him. There's a handful of sterling-silver jewelry too: a skull necklace, a clunky bracelet that connects to a snake ring. Garth's jewelry.

And Natalie's scarf—the one that she lent to me, the one I used for Parker's wounds. The bloodstains are still visible. Taylor's cell phone is here too. I'd left it behind at the amusement park; it's still in its leopard-print case.

I continue to pull things out: sheet music from Frankie, Shayla's square black glasses, Natalie's feather-capped pen—the one she used with her stationery. I reach in a little deeper, spotting something dark at the bottom of the trunk. I grab a piece of it, almost unable to digest what it truly is.

In my hand.

Between my fingers.

The jet-black color.

The coarse texture.

Natalie's wig.

It's like when someone dies at war—when they send home the remains in a box.

Tears run down my face. I slip the pendant necklace around my neck, hoping that, somehow, it was indeed my mother's touch I felt earlier, that she's watching over me somewhere, that she can give me the strength I need.

IVY

I STUFF SOME OF THE ITEMS FROM THE TRUNK INTO
my bag. And then I get up and shine my flashlight along the
walls, spotting an open doorway. It appears to lead downward,
deeper into the ground. There's a dripping sound somewhere—
leaking pipes? Creepy sound effects? I grab my knife again. My
hand wrapped tightly around it, I move down a stairwell—rock
slabs—feeling my pulse race.

The walls and ceiling are dirt, held in place with wood strap-
ping; it's as if a tunnel's been carved out of the earth. Candles

light up the ground, guiding the way, affirming the obvious: I'm supposed to be here.

There's a door at the end of the tunnel. I try the handle; it's locked. With trembling fingers, I pull both the key ring and the gold key out of my pocket. I try the gold key first and go to unlock the door, but I drop the key in the process. It falls to the ground. I scramble to pick it up, my fingers raking over the dirt. The key gripped between my fingers, I try again.

A second later, I hear it: a piercing scream that stabs right through my heart, nearly bringing me to my knees.

Taylor's scream.

The key's in the lock.

I get the lock to turn.

Where did her scream come from? Behind me? Beyond the door?

"Taylor?" I shout.

The door cracks open. There's a light on inside—another spotlight, maybe—but I'm unable to see much. Walls on both sides of the doorway block my view. I take a few steps to the end of the wall, finally able to look beyond it.

My heart hammers. My entire body tingles. The breath stops in my lungs.

Parker's here. In a cell. Lying on the ground.

His face is pale and gaunt. It doesn't look like he's breathing. He's wearing someone else's clothes: baggy sweats, a red T-shirt.

"Parker," I cry, but no sound comes out.

The room starts to spin. I hear a shifting noise behind me. I turn to look.

Natalie's face is pressed between two cell bars. She's staring straight at me. Her eyes are red. Her cheeks look hollow. Her wig is gone, leaving coarse, uneven hair: half a bang, lopsided length.

My mind reels with questions. Is it possible that the joke's on me? That her image will fade in a matter of moments? I blink hard, but still she remains.

She's real.

I'm here.

"You were warned," she mumbles; her voice is shallow and weak. "Harris warned you. He told me. I told you." She stumbles over her feet, seemingly unfazed by my presence. "Don't let her out of your sight. Is it true what Harris has been telling me, that Taylor came here too, that she's missing now as well? That she's not going to make it?"

"No," I whisper, shaking my head. "She's fine. Taylor will be fine."

Natalie covers her ears with her hands, as if Harris is speaking to her at this very moment.

"No," I repeat, studying her eyes. Beneath the redness, her pupils are dilated; there's only a slim ring of blue. "Were you given something?" I ask her, assuming she must've been sedated or tranquilized.

"Not as much as him." She nods to Parker. "But Harris warns me about that too—about which foods to eat and how much to drink."

It takes me a second to notice the lock at the front of the cell. I fish a key out of my pocket—the gold one again—and jam it into the lock, suspecting that it won't turn.

But it does. The lock clicks. The cell door swings open.

I hurry over to Parker's cell, fearing the key won't work, dropping it once again. It lands inside the cell. I scoot down and reach in, between the bars, but I can't quite get it. I need a few more inches. I struggle to reach in farther, my shoulder jammed against the bars, my cheek pressed against the dirt.

Finally, I'm able to grasp it. I get up and stick the key into the lock. It turns.

I'm in.

I rush over to Parker's side.

"Hurry," Natalie shouts.

I shake his shoulder and call out his name over and over. At last, I can tell he's breathing—can feel the air exhale out of his nostrils.

"He's been like that for a while," she says, joining me inside the cell.

I reach into my bag, retrieving a small tin box filled with lemongrass and peppermint tea leaves, along with a bottle of eucalyptus oil. I unscrew the cap off the oil, pour a few droplets over the leaves, and mix it all up with my finger, releasing the scent notes.

"What are you doing?" Natalie asks.

I place the tin in front of Parker's nose and wait for him to breathe it in. After a few moments, his eyes open.

He sees me.

His lips part.

He blinks a couple of times, perhaps thinking that this is a dream.

I pinch his forearm. "It's real," I tell him, leaning in to kiss his forehead.

Parker labors to sit up, lifting himself with his elbow and then his hand. His eyes are dilated too. "Ivy," he whispers; his voice is frail.

"Don't try to talk."

He reaches out to touch my face. His fingers are cold; they tremble against my skin. "You came back."

I nod, desperate to hold him, to touch him, to never let him go again.

He squeezes my hand. I recognize the fit of my palm inside his grip.

"We need to go," Natalie insists, looking toward the doorway.

Parker tries to get up, stumbling back, uneven on his feet.

"Stay close to me." I stand and take his hand. "We're going to get through this, but I need you to be strong for me."

We move down the tunnel and up the slab steps. Parker's gait is slow and clumsy. Back in the open basement area, something catches my eye—over to the side. There's something reaching out from the bottom of a closed door.

I move closer, my mind almost unable to grasp what I see.

Fingers.

Chipped green nail polish.

Taylor's hand.

There's a puddle of blood seeping through the crack at the bottom of the door, gushing beneath my shoes.

I try the knob. It's locked. The gold key doesn't work, neither do the keys on the ring. "Taylor!" I shout.

"She won't answer you," a voice says.

I look back at Parker and Natalie, standing a few feet behind me. But the voice didn't come from either of them. It came from someplace else—across the cellar, hidden in the shadows. I hear the scuffing of his boots.

"Hello, Princess," he says, stepping into the path of my flashlight beam.

The sight of him evokes a visceral reaction in my gut. I grab the knife from my bag.

"Taylor isn't the only one who didn't make it. Those who aren't currently present were properly disposed of long ago."

"No." I clench my teeth and shake my head.

"I couldn't let her get away twice, after all. You, Parker, Natalie— you three are my survivors. For now, anyway." He giggles.

He looks exactly as he did at the amusement park, wearing an elf mask (rosy cheeks, darted brows, and a perma-smile) and dressed in a bright red suit, floppy hat, and green gloves.

He cocks his head. His tongue peeks out through the mouthhole in the mask. "It's very nice to see you."

I lunge for him, knife first, picturing the tip of the blade puncturing his neck. I go to stab him, aiming for the area just above his collarbone.

He grabs my arm and twists it behind my back—a stinging, wrenching pain.

I bend forward, trying to break free and unwind from his grip.

"Feel nice?" he asks; I can hear the smile in his voice.

Parker comes at him, swinging at his face, hitting him square in the jaw. I topple to the floor, landing on my side.

311

The killer is quick to rebound, securing his mask, and then pushing against Parker's chest.

Parker nearly loses his balance, taking a moment to regain stability. He blinks a few times, confused.

"You're in no condition for such heroics," the killer says to him, pulling something from his pocket. A needle, with a syringe.

I charge him, wielding the knife above my head. But the killer trips me, winding his leg around mine, grinding his elbow into my spine. I hear a loud crack.

He shoves me, face-first. I land against my chest. The camera flies from my head. My nose hits the ground. The knife jumps from my grip. I go to retrieve it, blood pouring from my nose.

Parker jumps at the killer once more, throwing his weight against him, trying to knock him down. The killer staggers back a few steps, but then regains his footing. He thrusts Parker—hard.

Parker falls headfirst to the floor. He tries to get up, but the Nightmare Elf kicks him in the side—again and again and again—before jabbing the needle deep into Parker's thigh.

Parker lets out a sharp, piercing wail that stabs through my heart.

"No!" I scream.

Parker looks at me with a pleading expression—his eyes wide, his mouth parted. But, not two seconds later, those same eyes go vacant.

His legs stop twitching.

His body lies still.

"This is turning out better than I anticipated," the killer says, zeroing in on me again.

Still on the floor, I look around, searching for Natalie, but she's nowhere in sight. Where did she go?

The killer turns to face me, his head cocked to one side. "Your turn?" he asks, taking out another needle.

I get up and meet his eyes, noticing the motion of his chest as he breathes. He's slightly winded. His feet—work boots—are pointed toward me, ready to charge.

I wait for his first move, conjuring up various lessons I've learned in self-defense class: eye contact is key; timing is essential; more than half of all defense begins in the mind as we await the opponent's vulnerability.

I'm done being the vulnerable one.

He comes at me, the needle clenched in his fist, angling down toward my neck. I take a step back, watching the needle in my peripheral vision—just six inches from my heart now—anticipating the opportune moment.

I plunge the knife deep into his gut. The needle drops to the floor.

He retreats, but then unzips his coat, revealing a layer of protective padding strapped to his body. My knife's stuck inside the padding.

"Nice try, my Princess." He laughs. "But I'm always one step ahead." He grabs the handle of the knife and twists it left and right, trying to pry it out.

I run before he can, as fast as my legs will take me—hating myself for each stride I take toward the door, leaving Parker once again.

NATALIE

I BACK AWAY—SLOWLY AT FIRST—KEEPING MY EYE ON the fight.

Parker and the Elf.

Ivy and the Elf.

My fight is with Harris.

"I can't just leave like this," I tell him, able to hear tears in my voice.

"There's no other choice," Harris says. *"Not unless you want to be killed. A slice to your neck, in front of a mirror, so you can watch."*

Is he saying that just to scare me? The mirror detail is suspect, but I don't want to chance it.

When I get to the doorway, I turn and run down the stairs, headed for the bulkhead exit. I know it's here somewhere.

The hallway is dark, lined with candles along the ground, positioned every few feet. I grab a candle for light and then move in the opposite direction of where the prison cells are located, turning left and then going right, trying to stay focused on Harris's voice.

"There," Harris says, referring to a weathered door just a few feet away.

I remove the wooden brace across it. The door creaks open. A set of stairs faces me, but it's too dark. I can only make out two of the treads.

There's a slamming sound in the distance. It blows right through me, like a gunshot to my heart.

"What are you stopping for?" Harris asks.

I move up the stairs, into a black hole. My head hits something hard. Am I trapped? What's happening? Harris, are you still here?

I set the candle on a step and reach up. My fingers rake against something cold, hard, metal—like a ceiling above my head. I push upward, feeling a little give. My muscles quiver. My head whirs. I slip down a step. I don't think I can do this.

"You can," Harris tells me.

Using all my strength, I push harder. The bulkhead doors part open. A funnel of cold air blows against my face.

But then my muscles give. My arms jitter. I let out a wild animal cry.

Harris whispers in my ear: *"This is your only hope, your only chance."*

I take a deep breath and push upward again, punching against the metal, popping the doors open. They start to close once more, but I punch them again, feeling a rip in my skin. The doors splay open.

I climb up the rest of the stairs and take a step outside. The cold air kisses my face, finds the bald patches on my head, reminding me who I am.

But still, I'm out, I'm free.

"Not yet," Harris says.

Ivy

I CAN HEAR HIM COMING AFTER ME—THE CLOBBER OF his boots, the panting of his breath. I hurry down the hallway, my nose still bleeding, my shoulder aching from when he twisted my arm. I scan the walls, still looking for the photos of Frankie, Garth, and Shayla, as if they might possibly reappear.

In the lobby, there's a chair positioned dead center. Two dolls sit on it—a mama with a little boy. Both have cracked porcelain faces. The mama only has one cheek and half of a forehead. Their eyes are white, the pupils faded. The boy doll looks sad, its mouth turned downward. There's a tear inked onto its cheek.

"Leaving so soon?" the mama's voice squeaks out. *"I was just in the middle of telling a bedtime story."*

Facing the exit door, I feel a rush of adrenaline inside my veins, but I know that I can't leave—not now, not yet. I turn away, just as the killer appears. He stands in my flashlight's beam.

"Leaving so soon?" he asks. "The story isn't over yet."

"I want to see your face."

He's got the camera strapped to his head now. The shadow of a candle flame flickers across his mouth.

"Show me," I tell him, trying to be strong, hearing a quiver in my voice.

He shakes his head again. His tongue sticks out through the hole in the mask. He waggles it up and down, teasing me, taunting me.

Keeping my eyes on his, I take a deep breath, noticing the knife gripped in his hand, down by his side.

"Leaving so soon?" the doll asks again. *"I was just in the middle of telling a bedtime story."*

The killer comes at me with the knife, slicing through the air, releasing a maniacal scream.

I duck and pivot to the side. The knife punctures the door. I smash him over the head with my flashlight—so hard that the flashlight falls from my grip, crashes to the floor.

Using both hands, he tries to pry the blade from the wood.

At the same moment, I kick him—hard—my heel plunging into the back of his knee. He collapses forward, losing his grip on the knife. But still he rebounds quickly, catching himself on the floor. He goes for the knife again.

Meanwhile, I grab and twist the door handle, tearing the door wide open, smacking it against his head. I shiver at the impact—a deep clunk sound.

He lets out a howl. I hear him stumble back.

I snag my flashlight and plow down the front steps—three at time.

It's dark out. The chill in the air moves across my skin, waters my eyes. I run through the courtyard area, past the water fountain, headed for the woods, hoping the darkness can swallow me whole.

It's quiet behind me. Is he still in the building? Watching me from afar? I wind through the mazelike bushes and get back on the trail, moving forward, feeling as if I've gotten a decent lead.

I stop, click off my flashlight, and crouch down behind some bushes, desperate to know where he is, tempted to go back.

My pulse races. My body shivers. I don't hear him anywhere. I can't see a thing in the dark. Does he have a flashlight too?

After several moments, I stand and take a step. There's a loud snap. It echoes inside my bones, freezes me in place. It takes me a beat to realize that the sound was from me; I stepped on a stick.

"Leaving so soon?" a voice squeaks out, cutting the dark silence. It's the doll's voice, right behind my ear.

I let out a scream. Hands wrap around my neck. The knife is pressed against my throat. I can feel his chest against my back, can feel his breath against my skin.

"You'll always be my princess," he whispers, running the blade along my neck.

I swallow hard, my mind reeling, my heart pounding, waiting for the right moment. Wind rustles through the trees, sending shivers all over my skin.

I press my back closer to his chest. The motion takes him aback; I'm able to feel his sharp inhalation. Before he can blow it out, I pound him—hard—in the groin, with the flashlight.

The knife drops. He lets out a grunt and doubles over. I kick him again, plunging the heel of my shoe into his hip. He topples over, leaving me a window to run.

I grapple through the brush. Branches scrape my face, pull at my hair, slow me down. But I continue through them as best I can in the dark, keeping my bag in front of my eyes as a shield.

A good seven or eight strides away, I bump into something hard—a tree trunk. There's brush all around it. I maneuver past and take a few more steps.

"Come out, come out, wherever you are," the killer sings.

I stop in place, able to hear him moving toward me—the crunch of his boots over dirt, the sound of twigs snapping beneath his feet. But he isn't using a flashlight either, so I can't see him anywhere.

I crouch down, and wait, and listen. After several moments, his footsteps seem to veer off in another direction; I hear the sound of twigs snapping at least several yards away.

I click the flashlight on, keeping the beam angled low, searching for the path. I don't see it anywhere. I turn the flashlight off and venture to stand. It's quiet again; he must be standing still too.

There's a rustle in the brush; it sounds as if it's coming from a distance. I click the flashlight on again—for just a second—hoping to finally find the path.

Instead I find him—his eyes.

No mask.

My parents' killer.

He holds a flashlight at his chin, highlighting his face. "You got your wish. It's been a long time since you've seen this face, hasn't it, Princess? Did you miss it?" He's standing only a few feet away; we're separated by a sprawling bush.

I recognize his silver hair—thick and wiry. I picture him standing over my bed seven years ago—his dark gray eyes, his crooked teeth, the stubble on his chin, and the scar down his face.

"I would've stayed to tell you a bedtime story that night in your room, but our time was cut short, wasn't it, Princess?" He begins toward me again, the camera still strapped around his head, recording our every move. Part of me wants to charge right into him, but I try to bolt instead.

I barely get two steps before I feel myself pulled back. He yanks me by the hair, giving me a sharp tug, dragging me into some brush. There's a knife—a new one, with a jagged edge—pressed against my neck.

He's crouched behind me. I'm on my back. Razor-like branches poke beneath my clothes, cutting into my skin.

"I'd have told you the story about little Johnny and the burning house." He points the tip of the blade below my ear and makes a tiny incision. He draws the knife downward, toward my chin. I can feel a trickle of blood, can see a star-filled sky.

"Once upon a time," he begins, "a little b—"

There's a loud, hard thwack. Something metal. He lets out a wail and releases his hold on me. The knife falls from my neck.

I scramble to turn over, hearing the thwacking sound again.

Natalie's there, with a shovel in her hand. The killer is down on the ground. I shine my flashlight over a trickle of blood running from his forehead.

Natalie takes the killer's flashlight and points it beyond the brush, zeroing in on the path. "Come on," she says.

Together we run, swiping branches and brush from in front of our eyes. Eventually, after what has to be a couple miles, we get to the lake. The boat's there. We untie it from the stump and climb in. I grab the oar. My arms ache as I paddle.

Natalie keeps the flashlight pointed toward the dock on the other side of the lake. With her other arm, she paddles, as we steer in that direction. It feels like we're going nowhere. I can't paddle fast enough.

There's a giant splash sound. Natalie sits up straight, pulls her arm out of the water. Did he jump in? Is it another trick? I paddle harder; my arms move faster.

Finally on the other side, I scramble to climb out, nearly losing my balance. Already on the dock, I hold Natalie's forearm, and we struggle our way across the field.

I can tell she's weak, can see it in her gait. It's labored and clumsy; she's staggering from side to side. Her adrenaline's running out.

Her knee buckles slightly and she lets out a yelp. I secure her arm to catch her from falling. With each step, our pacing gets slower, heavier. We still haven't reached the rock wall. There's so much more distance to run. My wounded knee is aching.

"I can't," Natalie whines. She stops short, all out of breath, placing her hands down on her knees.

"You *can*," I insist, still holding on to her forearm, giving her a tug forward. "It's just a little bit farther," I lie.

But Natalie won't budge. She shakes her head and sinks to the ground. Tears run down her cheeks. I pull my water bottle out of my bag and kneel down beside her. I place the spout at her lips.

She takes a few sips, but then ends up hacking up. "Go without me."

"No. We've come too far."

She curls up on the grass. "Just leave me here to die. I don't really care. I miss Harris too much anyway."

"Harris won't be waiting for you," I tell her. "Not if you quit."

She looks at me, her eyes enlivened. "Has he been talking to you too?"

"He has," I lie. "Now, come on." I help her up, and we begin forward again, my knee throbbing with each step.

At last, we reach the rock wall. We climb over it and continue across the second field, not stopping until we get to the road where the bus let me out. My breath is visible—a long-winded puff of air. A mix of emotions stirs inside my heart: sorrow, failure, loss, relief.

I look down both sides of the road, spotting a car moving toward me in the distance. I flag it down. Natalie's sitting on the ground.

There's a young couple inside. A tiny black dog.

"Could you give us a ride to the police?" I ask, keeping a firm grip on my bottle pendant.

I think they say yes. Maybe I respond with a thank-you.

The couple asks us questions: if we're okay, what happened. Too much to answer. Way too much to think about.

Natalie opens the car door. There's a sweet tobacco scent inside the car. She scoots in to make room for me.

But I don't move. And I can barely breathe.

"Ivy?"

I look at the driver. She reminds me a little of Shayla—dark skin, pretty smile.

"Come on," Natalie says, patting the seat beside her.

"I can't," I tell her, shaking my head.

"Ivy—"

I close the car door and head back toward the field.

PARKER BRADLEY

INT. BASEMENT, ABANDONED GOTHIC
BUILDING-NIGHT

A large open space with cracked cement
floors and overhead ductwork. It's dark,
except for a spotlight that hangs in the far
corner, several yards away.

ANGLE ON ME

I lie on the ground in a pool of my own
blood. My head is bleeding. No one else is
here. I've got to leave too.

I manage to sit up, but I can't move my leg.
I can't even feel it.

Using all my strength, I prop myself up
on my elbows and slither across the floor,
toward the doorway that'll lead out.

I let out a GRUNT. My bones ache. My muscles
twitch. Drool drips down my chin.

En route to the doorway, there's a puddle of
blood on the floor, seeping out from a door
to the left.

CLOSE ON DOOR

A hand sticks out from beneath it, palm
facing up. The nails have chipped green
polish.

I go to reach up for the knob, but my elbow
buckles and I nearly fall on my face. I try
again, sitting up. The door is locked, as
before. The wood is thick and heavy. I'd
need to be able to stand to bust it open.

I POUND on the door.

                    ME
          Hello? Can you hear me?

I touch the fingers. The skin is cold. I
apply pressure to the thumb, looking for a
response. There isn't one; no movement—even
when I pinch the skin.

I continue to POUND on the door, shoving my
weight against it as best I can in a seated
position, continuing to SHOUT for whoever's
inside to hear me.

A door SLAMS somewhere. I stop pounding
and drop down to the ground. On my elbows

again, I slither along the floor, working my way to the doorway. The skin on my forearms burns.

There are FOOTSTEPS in the distance. I'm just a few feet from the doorway now. A trickle of sweat runs from my forehead.

I wrestle my way down the slab steps, landing face-first. My chin hits a rock. My teeth clank together. Blood runs from my nose. I drag myself onto the dirt floor; it's lit up with candles that lead the way back to the prison cells.

I move to the left, through an open doorway. My shirt rolls upward. The skin on my stomach scrapes against something sharp—a tearing, singeing pain—and I wince.

It's completely dark here. No lights, no candles. I continue to crawl forward, my fingers raking over the dirt. My fingers are raw and bleeding.

The ground feels suddenly colder. I must be getting closer. A door hinge WHINES somewhere. There are other sounds too: CLANKING, BANGING, CLAMORING, the RUSTLING of bags.

I keep moving forward, unable to see a thing. I should've grabbed a candle. It's too late to turn back now.

I hit a dead end—a dirt wall. I move in the opposite direction. Another dead end. The FOOTSTEPS move in my direction. I don't know where to go. I back up against the wall, praying that he won't find me.

IVY

I RUN ACROSS THE FIELD AND CLIMB BACK OVER THE rock wall, wondering how much time has passed since I left Parker. It has to be well over two hours (no less than forty-five minutes in the woods with the killer; another ninety minutes, at least, getting to the street with Natalie; and now an additional hour to get back). There's a cramp in my side. It bites below my ribs, nagging me to stop.

Finally I get to the lake, but the boat has floated away. I can see it in the distance—too far to swim. The oar has floated off as well—in the opposite direction than the boat.

I kick off my shoes, not knowing what to do with my flashlight. I search inside my bag, pulling out the Ziploc I use to store my mix of tea leaves. I dump the tea onto the ground and then slip the flashlight inside the bag. It doesn't fit. The handle's about two inches too long. I zip the bag up as best I can and fasten a rubber band around it. Then, I toss my shoulder bag to the side.

Keeping hold of the flashlight, I dive in. The water chills me to the bone, shocks my entire body. I begin my way across, trying to swim as fast as I can without making too much of a splash, but the other side of the lake looks so far away. My stomach aches. There's a gnawing sensation in my shoulder.

Treading water, I pause a moment to catch my breath, angling my flashlight at the other side of the lake. I'm only about halfway there.

I continue to paddle for several more minutes. My body feels like lead. My fingers are numb. I struggle through the water— flailing, kicking, swiping—trying to move as fast as I can while keeping the flashlight up. But for all the work, I can't get there quickly enough. I'm making too much of a splash. And my flashlight's getting wet.

A few strokes later, something stops me in my path. A thick, slimy substance. I try to get through it, but it's all around me, weighing me down, twisting around my ankles—ribbons of something slippery—pulling at my feet.

I struggle forward, flashing back to Parker's nightmare—the eels that swarmed him. But whatever this is, it doesn't seem like it's alive. Could it be algae? Do lakes have their own form of seaweed? Did the killer dump something into the water?

I fall beneath the surface, still struggling to hold the flashlight upward. Water fills my nose, my ears; it leaks between my teeth. Something gritty slides down the back of my tongue. I make my way upward, able to see something floating all around me; it catches in the light. Thick bands of something dark.

I splash forward, concentrating on the muscles in my legs, channeling more mantras from self-defense: *I'm stronger than what weighs me down. I can get past that which tries to anchor me.* I thwart the slime to the side. It catches on my arm. I shine my flashlight over it. A dark olive goop. It doesn't look real.

The other side of the lake is still several yards away. I continue to paddle toward it, finally free of the muck. At last I reach the bankside. Breathing hard, I climb out, collapsing to the ground. My wounded knee stings.

My flashlight blinks. The inside must've gotten wet. Angling it outward, I get up and run down the path that cuts through the woods, my bare feet trampling over dirt and rocks. Branches and brush cut into my face, pull at my hair. I'm shivering. My teeth chatter. The flashlight continues to blink.

I trip and fall forward again. My cheek lands against something sharp. I touch the spot. The wound is open. I can feel a gash in my skin. Blood comes away on my hand.

I go to rip a piece of fabric from the scarf on my knee, noticing the blood that's seeped through the fabric. It's sopping wet.

Meanwhile, blood runs down my neck. My fingers quiver over the spot. A whimper escapes out my mouth.

I bring the collar of my sweatshirt upward to catch the blood. Then I continue to move forward again. The school must be close.

I wind through the maze of bushes, panting the whole way. Is the killer still in these woods? Is he watching me? Did he go back inside? Am I already too late?

I stumble forward, over a rock, but catch myself before I fall. Still, I step down on something pointed. A ripping, burning pain sears my skin and radiates up my calf.

Wind whirs through the trees, rustles the branches. Sticks break somewhere behind me. I turn the flashlight off, squat down, and wait, and listen.

"Ivy?" a male voice whispers.

I grab a sharp stick and try my best to stand. My foot aches. My knee stings. My head feels dizzy as I struggle to my feet. I grip the stick hard, confident that his voice is coming from an area to my left.

I click on my flashlight, ready to strike out. The beam blinks a couple times before I'm able to see.

His eyes stare back at me in the light, taking my breath. He's lying on the ground. Blood runs from his forehead.

Parker.

I race to him. His face looks pale. He's shivering uncontrollably. "Just hold on," I tell him, using the hem of my shirt to blot his wound. "Do you think you can walk?"

"My leg," he croaks out. "I can't move it."

I touch right above his knee. His leg twitches in response. I do the same to the other one, but nothing happens. "Is that the one he injected?" I ask, putting the pieces together.

I blanket myself over him, placing my hand over his heart. I can't feel a beat, but his breath is at my neck. "We're going to get through this." I kiss his cheek. His skin is cold. I look in the direction of the school. It must be so close now. "I should go back for the others too."

"There aren't any others." His eyes close.

The flashlight goes out completely.

"Just hold on," I tell him, my mind scrambling, trying to decide what to do. Go back to look for Taylor? Run to get help?

I take his hand to feel his pulse. At the same moment, sirens sound in the distance, giving me breath. I collapse onto his chest, praying that by some miracle Taylor will be okay.

PARKER

ONE DAY LATER

FADE IN:

INT. HOSPITAL—THE FOLLOWING DAY

A typical hospital room with stark white
walls and a TV that hangs from the ceiling.

ANGLE ON ME

I lie in bed, attached to all sorts of
machines and monitors that ensure everyone
that I'm okay. There are stitches in my head
and bandages all over my body. A bag of
fluid is being fed to me intravenously.

I look like shit—sallow from lack of
sunlight and thirty pounds skinnier than I
used to be, pre-Dark House weekend.

PULL BACK TO REVEAL IVY

She sits by my side, resting her head down
on my chest. I squeeze her hand to let her
know that I'm awake.

She looks up. She's wearing a T-shirt and
sweatpants, her hair's pulled back in a
long ponytail. She looks unbelievably
amazing.

                    IVY
        How are you feeling?

                    ME
     I could ask you the same.

She's a patient here too, and has been
bandaged up accordingly—knee, foot,
shoulder, chin. And while I'm pretty sure
visitation for me only includes family, the
rules have been bent for those who risk
their lives to save people they barely know.

                    IVY
     As well as can be expected, I guess.
     Without Taylor. Without the others.

                    ME
     You saved my life. You saved Natalie's
     too. You brought the police closer to
     finding the killer.

She nods, listening to the words, but I'm
not sure she truly hears them. There's a
sadness in her eyes, an absence in her whole
demeanor.

                    IVY
Apple slept by my bed last night. Your
parents are on their way too. Someone
said the plane landed about an hour
ago. It must be pretty surreal . . . the
idea of seeing them after all this
time.

                    ME
The whole thing's surreal.

                    IVY
You still haven't told me how you
managed to get out of the basement.

                    ME
With only one working leg? Imagine a
snake with elbows.

                    IVY
Through the front door?

I shake my head.

                    ME
Through a side door he liked to use—
sort of like a bulkhead. I used to sit
in my cell, tensing when I heard the
bolts unlatch on his way in. And then
I'd hold my breath, waiting to hear him
lock back up: the cold, hard clank of
metal against metal.
                (looking away)
I don't really want to think about it.

My heart monitor speeds up. I take a deep
breath, trying to put stuff out of my
mind.

                    IVY
The police will be asking you.

                    ME
Someone was in already. They said I'll
be getting released soon. I can hardly
wait to fly back home, see the rest of
my family, my friends . . .

                    IVY
              (faking a smile)
That's great.

                    ME
But I'm coming back, Ivy. That's *my*
promise to you. I want us to begin
again.

                    IVY
You don't have to promise anything
right now.

                    ME
I want to. The time we've spent
together . . . I know it hasn't been
much, but I feel you know me in a way
that no one else ever could.

                    IVY
I suppose I do.

ME

So, then will you let me come back?
You don't have to say anything right
now. Because I know you've probably
moved on, met new people, got your
life back on—

Before I can finish babbling, Ivy leans
forward and shushes me with a kiss. My
heart monitor speeds up again. But instead
of trying to tame it, I pull her closer,
confident that I'll never let go.

CUT TO:

NATALIE

MY PARENTS SHAKE THEIR HEADS AT THE SIGHT OF me, lying in my hospital bed, in my hospital gown and bandages. I feel like I've been away for years, traveled over a million miles, and yet they still look at me as they always did—like I'm their biggest disappointment.

"I told you that contest was a bad idea," my father says, standing at the foot of the bed. "You could've gotten yourself killed."

My mother props an extra pillow behind my head. Her eyes linger on my patchwork scalp. I want to pull out more hair, but

I hold in the impulse by taking a deep breath and focusing on a blotch on the ceiling.

"It must've been so scary for you," she says.

"It was, but I had Harris to keep me company. I would never have survived without him."

"Harris is dead," my father barks. "His body was buried inside the ground."

"No, he's alive." I shake my head. "His soul is cradled inside my heart."

Dad turns his back, unable to look at me now. Meanwhile, Mom remains on the sidelines—mute, pretty, obedient—in her pale blue dress, with the matching bag. But still her eyes look swollen, like she hasn't slept. And I'll bet those are unspoken words on her parted lips.

"You haven't learned anything, have you?" Dad asks me.

"I've learned that I don't need others to believe me—to validate what I know in my heart to be true." I take another big breath, focusing again on the blotch, breathing through the impulse to pull.

"*I wish you really believed that,*" Harris says. "*Hopefully, in time you will.*"

Mom opens a bag she's brought along. Butternut squash soup, my sister Margie's favorite, which means that I must like it too.

"Where's Margie?" I ask.

"She couldn't get away," Mom says. "Too busy with her studies. She made highest honors this term."

Dad sighs. Because I never made honors? Because my being here means he had to take time off from work, and pay for airfare and a hotel? "How long do they want you in here?" he asks.

His question makes my eyes fill. He doesn't seem happy to see me. And I can't live in this hospital forever, where the nurses call me a hero. I'll be released in only a couple of days.

Mom takes the cover off the soup and sets it down on a tray. "Eat this," she says, as if it could possibly make everything better.

There's a rap on the door. A woman with dark purple hair appears. "Natalie?" she asks, glancing at both of my parents, silently asking permission to come in. "I'm probably breaking the visitation rules, but . . . my name is Apple. I'm Ivy's mother." She bypasses my parents when they don't respond, and sits down on the chair beside my bed. "You must be thrilled to see your daughter," she says to them.

Mom musters a polite smile, as if this moment is at all smile-worthy, while Dad merely clears his throat.

"Mom and Dad love you," Harris says. *"They just don't know how to show it."*

Apple takes my hand. Her fingers are warm. She smells like oranges. "You saved my daughter's life. Ivy tells me that if it weren't for you, she'd have never made it out of there." Her eyes locked on mine, tears of gratitude trickle down her cheeks. She leans in to kiss my forehead. Her palm glides over the crown of my head. "Thank you," she says, without a second glance to my hair.

I want to tell her how strong Ivy is; that if it weren't for her, I wouldn't be here either. But I'm crying too hard to speak. Her kindness is too much to bear.

I peer over her shoulder at my parents. My tears have made everything blurry, but somehow, despite the blur, things are starting to look a whole lot clearer.

Ivy

TWO WEEKS LATER

THE DOORBELL RINGS. IT'S APPLE AND CORE, bring-
ing me bags full of groceries. They've been stopping by at least
a couple of times a day to check on me. I can't really say I blame
them. My apartment is under twenty-four-hour surveillance,
because I saw the killer's face—again.

I've been racking my brain as to why he might've revealed it.
Was it because he thought he'd won—because he was convinced

he was going to kill me? Or maybe it was his twisted way of trying to reward me for a job well done.

Whatever the reason, I don't think he's going to come after me—at least not for a while anyway. The killer spent years of his life studying me—my choices, my psychology. But I'm no longer the same person. These past several months have changed me. If he wanted to come after me again, he'd need to discover this new person I've become.

"How are you doing today?" Apple asks, sitting across from me on the sofa. Her crumpled expression tells me that she already knows the answer.

"I'm okay," I lie. "I want to go back to work."

"Are you sure?" Her dark eyes narrow. "Maybe it's best to wait a few more weeks."

"I'm ready." I need the money. I need to appear normal. I need to show the killer that he didn't get the best of me.

"Miko's been asking about you." She runs her hand over her freshly cut hair spikes. She recently hacked off more than ten inches for Locks of Love. "I think he might have a crush."

"I wouldn't be so sure." Most people are calling me crazy for going after a killer with little more than a knife. Others are calling me selfish—myself included—for getting Taylor involved. I'm not sure how I'll ever forgive myself for letting her come along.

"I wouldn't be so *unsure* either." Apple winks.

I love Apple, and I know she means well, but the fact that she thinks I can move on after everything that's happened just distances us more.

After Parker and I were saved, the police scoped out the August Prep building, but they couldn't find any traces of Shayla, Frankie, or Garth—aside from the items left in the trunk. The blood I saw seeping through the door crack in the basement indeed belonged to Taylor, but, like the others, she was nowhere to be found.

What they *were* able to find? A bunch of the audio and video equipment, but none of the footage from that day. The killer had obviously been in a rush, but he knew just what to take. And, in the end, he got what he wanted—his sequel, right down to the final chase scene where the heroine faced her opponent.

The school's become a crime scene, not to mention a hot spot for Dark House series fans seeking a little thrill, eager to learn more about the legend of Ricky Slater. The good news: Though they won't reveal his identity, the police assure me that they know who the killer is. Now it's just a matter of finding him.

The police also have Natalie's testimony—for whatever it's worth. She claims that Parker was the only other survivor she saw during her time in captivity, and that, according to Harris, the bodies of Frankie, Shayla, and Garth are buried in a sinkhole somewhere in South Dakota. "Taylor's body will be dumped too," she told police. "That is if you don't find it first; Harris doesn't think you will."

Even though, so far, Harris has proven correct on pretty much all accounts, I'm still holding on to hope, praying that the others are somewhere out there still.

Core lifts a pot of something heavy onto the stove. "Apple and I stopped by the diner earlier," he says. "Miko made you a batch of his famous chicken gumbo soup."

"I'll have to call him to say thank you." I force a smile—and not because I don't think the gesture was incredibly sweet. I'm just not sure I'm capable of spontaneous smiles anymore.

"Dr. Donna called the house earlier," Apple says. "She'd love to start seeing you again."

"I'll call her too." I smile wider. The irony: I was never into acting before, but ever since the Dark House weekend, it's become a way of life—a means of survival even.

I move to the kitchen table and eat a bowlful of soup, forcing down each bite, hoping I'm playing a convincing role.

Once they finally leave, I head into the bedroom. Beside my bed is the box of letters from Parker. After the police found Parker and me in the woods, I asked an officer to go back to the lake for my bag. I gave the officer the items I took from the trunk: Garth's skull necklace, Shayla's glasses, Frankie's sheet music, Natalie's scarf and wig. But I kept Parker's box of letters for myself, because I didn't want it to get taken away.

Parker has my letters too—the ones I wrote to him and mailed to myself. I packaged them all up before he flew back home. We've been talking every night since he left, and texting a few times a day. He says he can't wait to get back here and see me again. Part of me can't wait either—the part that still holds on to hope.

I sit down on the edge of my bed and run his bracelet over my cheek, remembering our first kiss—on the deck, holding hands, facing one another; the warmth of his breath against my skin, a hot buttery heat spilling across my thighs.

I gaze at the wall—at the giant, mural-size posters (cityscapes of Paris and Nice) that hang from a curtain rod I was able to rig. I get up and unclip them, revealing hundreds of pieces of paper—maps and charts and graphs I've made; a wall covered in conclusions I've drawn, questions I have, facts I know, pictures I've found, hours I've spent trying to get into the mind of a killer.

He may be a step ahead right now, but he won't be for long. The heroine always wins in the end.

The End

EPILOGUE

SPRING

Ivy

I'VE TAKEN UP RUNNING AS A WAY TO CLEAR MY head—perhaps the very best form of therapy. When I'm running, there's nothing else. My thoughts clear. My worries flee. With the wind combing through my hair and the warmth of the sun against my cheeks, I imagine myself like an animal—wild, free, unstoppable.

My birth mother often joins me on my runs. I know that probably sounds crazy, but sometimes I'm even able to catch a hint of her lilac perfume. She may've passed on seven years ago, but she's never far from my side—I know that now. The Nightmare Elf was right about one thing: sometimes it's the things that scare us most that teach us the biggest lessons.

I inhale the smells around me—of freshly cut grass, morning rain, tree bark, and lilacs—and I listen to the birds chirp. It's only when I feel my legs betray me that I start to head back.

I'm just about home now. My aunt's car is parked in the driveway. She hasn't left for work yet. I slow my pace, moving up the walkway, noticing a large envelope sticking out from my mailbox. I take it. My name and address are printed across the front. It was postmarked in Canada, but there's no return address.

I unlock the door to my apartment and then lock it back up—three bolts, plus a chain, and a chair propped beneath the knob.

I unload the pockets of my jacket first—chewing gum, pepper spray, a knife, my cell phone—and then I sit down on the edge of the couch and tear the envelope open.

There's a book inside. It's navy blue, hardcover, with a torn spine and gold trim. My heart begins to pound, because I've seen this book before—in Ricky's room, on the bedside table, when I left the suicide note.

There's a tiny lock for a key.

I reach into my bag and search for the key ring from that night; I've been keeping it tucked inside a zippered compartment. I pluck it out and insert the smaller key into the lock. It turns. I open it up. The words THE PROPERTY OF E.W. GRADE 7, AUGUST PREPARATORY SCHOOL are printed on the inside cover.

The doorbell rings.

I look toward the windows. The blinds are drawn. Apple and Core are at work. My aunt is going to be late if she hasn't already left. Who else could it be?

My pulse racing, I stuff the book beneath the sofa and go to the door. I peek through the peephole, almost unable to believe who's standing there, suitcase in tow.

I remove the chair, unlock the bolts, retract the chain, and open the door wide.

"Hey," Natalie says.

"Hey." I smile—probably my first genuine one in weeks.

Natalie looks the best I've seen her yet. Her eyes are no longer red and swollen; they're a brilliant shade of blue, made more dramatic with inky-black lashes. Her hair is different too. It's been cut super-short, about an inch long all over.

Without another word, I move closer to give her a hug. Her arms wrap around my shoulders, and we melt into each other's embrace. There's so much I want to say—so much I need to know. Aside from a couple of texts back and forth to share our contact info, we haven't seen each other or spoken since the night of our escape (and our brief overlap at the hospital).

Our embrace breaks. Our eyes lock.

"What are you doing here?" I ask her. "Over a thousand miles from home."

"They just don't get me. I guess they never did. But that's okay." She shrugs. "I mean, I'll be okay."

I bite my lip, remembering calling her house during the Dark House weekend. Natalie's mother picked up, and when I told her how troubled Natalie was and asked for her understanding, all she gave me was anger and resentment.

"Do you think I could maybe stay here for a while?" The words come out shaky. Her face turns bright pink.

Maybe, like me, she isn't used to being vulnerable. And maybe, like her family, I don't understand her either. But still we share something pretty significant in common, and maybe that's more than enough for now. I take her bag and invite her inside.

ACKNOWLEDGMENTS

I WOULD FIRST LIKE TO THANK MY EDITOR, TRACEY Keevan, for her invaluable feedback and continuous enthusiasm for my work. I'm so grateful for her keen insight and enviable superpower of knowing just the right questions to ask. This book is so much stronger because of her.

A million thanks to my amazingly talented agent, Kathryn Green, for her literary guidance and advice, and for her willingness to discuss reality TV with me. Eleven books together later, I'm enormously grateful for all she does.

Special thanks to Scott Olson, my psychological guru, for

answering all of my questions pertaining to mental health and therapy. Any related errors found within this novel are mine and mine alone.

Thanks to friends and family members who are a constant source of support, who give me the time to write, offer to read drafts of my work, and who don't mind if the house gets messy or if I declare take-out night for dinner because I'm too busy working.

And lastly, a very special thank-you goes to my readers, who continue to support my work and cheer me on from near and afar. Thank you for reading my books, entering my contests, attending my workshops, sending me letters and artwork, coming to my events, and making book-inspired videos. I've said it before and I'll say it again, and again, and again: I'm eternally grateful. You guys are the absolute best.

LAURIE FARIA STOLARZ

WELCOME TO THE DARK HOUSE